RESIDENTS

OF THE

DEEP

Marianne Villanueva

CONTENTS

DUMAGUETE

When Carlos's mother decided to take him to Dumaguete, on the other side of the island, he didn't question her. One day she said, we have to go, and they did, walking with their overnight bags to the bus station, whose uneven ground was pooled with muddy brown water in which he could detect shapes darting, tiny black minnows. He stumbled once or twice but his mother never paused or looked behind her and he hurried to catch up.

He wondered why she hadn't asked the driver to take them. Nanding had returned home after dropping off Carlos's father at the office. But his mother had asked the security guard to call them a cab. The cab driver had stared at his mother as they got in the back. Carlos wanted to hit him.

His mother had dressed carefully for the trip. She was wearing one of her floaty dresses, and high-heeled white sandals, the better to show off her toes, which were long and thin and elegant and nothing like Carlos's, who in almost everything had taken after his father.

We are going to Seven Seas Resort, his mother said. You will like it. They have a pool.

And Carlos did like it, but that was only after he had thrown up twice during the twelve-hour bus ride along a twisty, narrow road that hugged the sides of the steep mountain. Whenever Carlos looked out the window, he saw terrifying views of deep, wooded gorges and, occasionally, the glint of flashing water. A sour vomit smell clogged his mouth, his nostrils, and Carlos was deeply embarrassed.

None of the other passengers seemed to mind. The old woman behind them even leaned forward and handed his mother a couple of plastic bags.

The town itself was small and not at all like what he'd expected. There were no signal lights, and everyone rode around on motorbikes or tricycles. These roamed all over the city and made terrific, belching noises. Smoke poured from their exhaust pipes, marring the fresh air that blew in from the ocean.

One day, they visited a crocodile farm. Carlos was intrigued by the scaly creatures whose mouths opened astonishingly wide at the approach, as though manipulated by invisible hinges.

Another day they visited a large zoo near the central plaza. His mother walked around silently, apparently content, her eyes resting briefly on the animals in their cages, one was said to be the *tamaraw*, a horned beast that looked, to Carlos, like nothing so much as a very small water buffalo, with a black hide and two thick, curving horns.

On the fourth day, Carlos felt his insides contract. His mother had taken him to the green campus of Silliman University. There, among the tall, old acacia trees, they'd stumbled across a small museum that held shells and voodoo charms from another small island, a short boat ride away: Siquijor, whose faint outline was just visible from Dumaguete's seaside promenade. All day, outrigger canoes transporting shells for selling to tourists plied the distance between the two islands. For years, Carlos had heard stories about this island, but his mother showed no inclination to go there.

Back home, his *yaya*, Dulce, had told him about witches, about the *manunungod* who hides under the floor of the room of a sick person, causing the patient to toss and turn feverishly. She had told him about *aswang*, creatures with long tongues who suck babies from the stomachs of pregnant women.

Dulce slept on a straw mat on the floor of his room. She only told him these stories when it was late and she was sure Carlos's father was asleep. Looking at the blackened implements in the Silliman Museum, he was suddenly reminded of the yaya and of her strangely urgent whisperings. And almost at the same instant, a picture of his room rose up in his memory: the Matchbox cars neatly arranged on the shelves, the navy-blue bedspread. Ma, he said, quite without thinking, I miss Papa.

Shush, his mother said. Stop being such a baby.

Will I ever see him again, Carlos asked, and to his horror tears began to well up in his eyes.

Of course you will, his mother said, patting his shoulder. Her hand was cool. He could feel the imprint of its coolness on the back of his T-shirt. It felt good.

Of course you will, his mother repeated, looking intently into his eyes. And Carlos was once again caught in that gaze, that green-eyed gaze that seemed to speak of nothing so much as time and sadness. He didn't know why his mother should have green eyes, when all his classmates' mothers had brown; why she didn't seem to love his father and threatened to leave him after every argument.

This was the first time she had taken him with her, though. Carlos had expected they would catch the next flight to Manila, where his grandparents lived. But instead, his mother had taken him to this strange city where they knew no one.

On the fifth or sixth day, a change seemed to come over his mother. Alert as he was to her ever-shifting moods, he sensed the change in her almost immediately. She seemed distracted, found excuses to leave him and go to the hotel lobby. Once, when he was swimming in the pool, he looked up and she was no longer in the deck chair that she'd dragged over to the shallow end, where he could look up from time to time and watch her reading her book (*A Journey of One Hundred Years*—what kind of title was that? It was not a book he would ever want to read.). When his mother was reading, two deep lines appeared on either side of her mouth, and she didn't look pretty anymore. For that reason, Carlos tried to call out to her and distract her, splashing energetically and making sure a few drops of water landed on her still form.

Now, when he looked up, she was gone. He felt a familiar panic rising. He feared she had left the hotel, that she might even have left the city. Now, Carlos was sure he was all alone. Now he must get his things and find his way back to his father, who lived all the way on the other side of the island.

Two days before, a group of men had come to stay at the hotel. They were large, stout men, with leathery skin and loud voices. They made the waitresses bring tray after tray of beer. They sat hunched over their restaurant table, telling stories about women and laughing.

It was the thought of these recent visitors that made Carlos finally get out of the pool, almost tripping over his towel in his haste. He noticed his mother had left her book, face down, on the ground beside the deck chair. One of the stout men who had arrived a few nights ago was sunning himself on a towel, some distance away. Carlos couldn't be sure, but he felt that the man had been watching him. This angered him; he tried to stare the man down, which was difficult since the man was wearing shades that reflected a deep, bronze sheen.

Carlos picked up his mother's book—he felt sure that the man would paw through it otherwise—and hurried to the cottage he and his mother shared, set some way back from the pool. He stepped on the veranda and noticed that his mother's slippers were gone. He opened the door to their room—by this time everything was swimming painfully in his head and he had a headache and a whoosh of cold air from the air-conditioner disconcerted him. The room was frigid. The beds were as they had been when he and his mother had left that morning, bringing their towels and their sunblock and her book. He went to the bathroom and saw her toiletries—brush, perfume bottle, lipstick—arranged neatly on the right side of the vanity. His mother had been laughing that morning, she had been happy. But Carlos had not returned her gaiety. He had remained silent in response to all her jibing.

He flipped the light on. In the harsh, fluorescent glare, he saw himself in the mirror. Who was this stranger peering back at him with a frightened expression? It was certainly not he, for he always felt he knew how to hide his emotions. It was a skill his mother lacked, and he had realized this about her very early. And he had carefully tended to his face, even when he was startled, even when he felt lost.

Now, however, the mirror made him call out.

Ma, he said. And then, more strongly, Ma!

He was aware that his own mother could not hear him, that she was far away, and he realized, with frightening clarity, that he was nothing but a child. He had loved it when, on his ninth birthday, almost a year ago, his father had surprised him with a party. It had been wonderful, for his mother had worn a white dress and held his father's hand and they had talked to each other in loving tones.

After, his mother had gone away for a much longer time than usual. Carlos felt her absence much more keenly this time. Yet he had no one, not even a brother or sister with whom he could share his grief, his terror. It had always been like this. Whenever his mother disappeared mysteriously from his life, as she had been doing more and more often in the past year, Carlos felt adrift. The reality of school, his friends, even his father, were no consolation for his loss.

His father would sneer hatefully at him. Grow up, he would say. Your mother is not coming back.

The days would pass in a long string of waiting.

Carlos's father was named Oscar. When Carlos's mother was away, another woman would come by the house. She had a deep, throaty laugh and wore colorful, high-heeled shoes that matched whatever dress she happened to be wearing.

Once, when this woman had bent to hug Carlos, he smelled his mother's perfume. The perfume his father had brought from Paris after a business trip that had made his mother clap her hands and cry out with surprise and pleasure.

The other woman's name, he found out, was Rica. Carlos observed how his father's voice would drop when he said Rica's name. Rica had children, but her husband, Carlos learned from his *yaya*, who seemed angry at the woman and angrier even at Carlos's father, had moved to the States and was already living with another woman there, even before the marriage had been officially annulled. The sad thing was that he had taken Rica's two young sons with him. Now she had no one—no one, that is, except for Oscar, Carlos's father.

"Your father is a prince," Rica had said once to Carlos. For a brief moment, Carlos's chest had swelled with pride. But, with his very next breath, he was conscious of somehow having betrayed his mother. In response to Rica's remark, Carlos had merely shrugged. Rica had given him a strange look. Then she had laughed and walked away.

Carlos daydreamed of ways to chase Rica from his father. He had come very close to writing her a note, to tell her that she must follow her husband, but he feared provoking his father's wrath. Instead, he waited silently, begging, pleading with his mother in his thoughts. And, each time, it seemed that his mother did hear him because, from whatever place she happened to be in, Carlos's mother would return. He would come down to breakfast one day and see her sitting demurely at the table, her hair damp and smelling clean and fresh, as if she had lingered among flowers. It was only then, at the moment of her return, that Carlos knew his heart had been broken. The pain was so real that he found it impossible to eat. It was as if his mother and father had each taken knives and plunged them into his very being. He, the fulcrum of these two opposing forces, could scarcely move or think and wanted only to die from exhaustion, the exhaustion of loving two people who felt only bitterness.

Carlos would often ask himself why his mother and father could not be happy. Or even *pretend* to be happy, for his sake. He dreamt that Rica assumed the shape of a fantastic, plumed bird. In her outstretched wings, she cradled his father's sleeping form. Other times, he dreamt of his mother, or at least of a being he felt to be his mother, though this woman was stooped and had white hair. In his dreams, his fragile, old mother moved about restlessly, tapping the floors with a wooden cane and then bending low as if listening for a sound from under the floorboards. Once she lifted it and hit a boy lurking in the shadows. Carlos cried out and felt pain shoot up his right arm. When he woke in the morning, the inside of his right elbow was bruised. Perhaps, he mused, he was a shapeshifter who visited others in his dreams.

The only thing that made Carlos feel better, after having had such a dream, was the voice of his *yaya*. Carlos didn't know how old Dulce was, but she was very old. She had come to the family with Carlos's mother. When Carlos's mother was not around, it was Dulce who talked to him, and told him stories at night, and made sure he ate his dinner. Sometimes Dulce looked at him and shook her head sadly. Then Carlos wondered what he had done. He dreamed of his mother, always.

Once his mother told him she had been in Costa Rica. He had felt anguish at this knowledge, at the wounding thought that his mother had boarded a plane, that she had flown many thousands of miles away from him, without a second thought.

His mother had looked at him expectantly, and after a few moments he realized she was waiting for him to ask a question, and he finally asked her what she had enjoyed most (when all the while he needed all the force of his will to tamp down his anger) and she had said, "The birds."

She then talked about the scenery, and how long it had taken to get to this beach and that, and how she was finally able to practice her Spanish, which had grown rusty from disuse. She described the friendliness of the people, their lustrous eyes and brown skin. The food, too, she had fallen in love with. The *callo pinto*—rice and black beans—with every meal; the fat, juicy watermelons, the papayas, the piña, the fried plantains; the grilled chicken; the picadillo de chayote with cilantro. And she had fallen in love with her inn, which was on some street whose name she couldn't remember but was only a block away from the Ministry of Tourism. His mother said she loved the way everyone would say, "*No te preoccupe*," which was now her favorite expression.

And, while his mother was describing all these things for him—she had no pictures, she never took a camera anywhere—Carlos, too, began to see in his mind the beautiful, clean country and the smiling, unworried people. He thought it must be like paradise, where he expected to go one day, and even though some part of him knew that his mother could not be trusted, that some of what she was telling him was not absolutely real, he understood why she had chosen to leave out details here and there. The world was a messy place that his mother wanted no part of. But here, with Carlos, she had invented an idea of a place where it was possible to be perfectly happy. The invention would always be their secret, a gift she shared only with Carlos.

He did not ask her whether she had told anyone that she was married and had a son. He guessed that his mother might not want to offer this information, not willingly. And anyway, she was over *there,* where no one knew her and where she must have felt she could start afresh. It was cruel, then, of him to have called her back, though he had had to do it; he simply couldn't live without her.

Carlos was thinking, remembering all these things as he left the frigid room and headed towards the main building where the reception desk was. He had to skirt a grove of coconut trees, and he noticed for the first time that he had seen no birds in this place, and he wondered whether it might be possible for him one day to see Costa Rica, his mother's beautiful paradise, for himself.

His mother didn't know, and he'd make sure she never knew, that in the last year he had learned how to smoke, filching a cigarette a week from the packs his father left on his dresser. He would take the precious stick to a secluded spot in their garden where, hidden behind a large *balete* tree, he would light it and practice breathing slowly, in and out, watching the smoke curl luxuriantly in the air above him. Sometimes he would deepen his voice and imitate his father. It made him feel big and proud to walk with his head held high and cocked to one side, the cigarette dangling from a corner of his mouth. Sometimes Carlos imagined it was *he* who held Rica, he who Rica gazed at with longing. And he could hardly wait until the day when he, too, could buy presents for pretty women and make them laugh.

The men were loud tonight. He could hear them, laughing and talking in the restaurant. The waitresses scurried around with frightened faces. The loudest of the men was puffing on a big cigar. He wore dark glasses, even in the gloom of the restaurant. He had a pistol tucked against his bulging stomach, in the waistband of his tight khaki pants. The others called him "Sir."

Carlos could feel Sir watching him as he entered the restaurant. Perhaps he'd been watching him a long time already. It was hard to tell, behind the opaque glasses. Carlos skirted his table carefully, but a heavy, dark hand shot out and Carlos, feeling the heavy pressure against his chest, stopped.

"*Teka muna*," the man said. He was smiling. "I want to ask you something." Carlos noticed the flash of gold on one of his teeth.

Carlos shook his head. He wished he could pretend he was deaf-mute. He'd done this, sometimes, and sometimes it had worked. Sometimes, when his teachers asked him a question he didn't know how to answer, he rolled his eyes and stuck out his tongue. This made his math teacher, in particular, increasingly angry. Finally, the teacher had thrown a blackboard eraser at him and ordered him out of the classroom. Carlos had moved slowly among the desks, as if underwater.

Sir kept his paw against Carlos's thin chest, and suddenly Carlos felt like crying. He turned his head, looking around for his mother, and Sir said, "Where is she?"

Carlos shrugged.

"The two of you come here by yourselves?" Sir asked. "Where is your father?" He pronounced it Pa-DERR; it was clear to Carlos that Sir was not an educated man. But this knowledge only increased his unease, and he flushed bright red. Then, he raised his shoulders and shrugged, miming an *I don't know.*

He raised both palms to the air. A hiccup of fear rose to his throat and before he could stop it, it emerged sounding like a belch. Sir laughed.

"What happened to you, *ha*, boy? I hear you talking to your mom, so I know you're not deaf or dumb. Maybe just scared, *ha*? Scared of Mario?"

Carlos mimed again, desperately rolling his eyes and shrugging. Sir stopped laughing and gazed at him through narrowed eyes. He'd tired of the game, Carlos could feel it, but he didn't know what else to do. He stood there, waiting.

Sir gave him a slight push, and Carlos, off balance, stumbled. Sir laughed, and the other men laughed, too. Carlos's face was burning. He faced the men.

"My father is coming," Carlos said. "He is coming."

But saying these words caused a kind of panic to rise in him. He realized, for the first time, that they really were alone there, he and his mother. He wondered why they were there at all, in that place so far from home, surrounded by strangers. And he wondered why his father had let them go, why his father was always letting them go, why he was never around at the moment of Carlos's greatest need. Such as now.

Perhaps it was the woman in the red dress, the one who came over when Carlos's mother was away. Perhaps she was the cause of his mother's unhappiness and ruin.

As he walked away, forcing himself to move slowly, Carlos heard Sir saying something to the others. He caught the word *puki* and the evil in their laughter. His heart was racing by the time he reached their cottage.

He flung open the door. His mother was on the bed, doing a crossword puzzle. She was wearing a loose, blue shift, and her hair was tied back from her face in a ponytail. She looked fresh and rested. She looked up when he entered and smiled.

"Where were you?" she said, as if she had been sitting there all this time.

Carlos sat on the bed.

"I want to go home," he said. He meant, *I want to go to my father.* She knew that was what he meant. Her face grew cold.

"No, not yet," she said. After a moment, she continued, "Aren't you having fun here? The food is good, no? I saw you eat so many mangos this morning."

"I don't care about mangos!" Carlos suddenly screamed.

His mother's arms encircled him almost immediately, but he would not be comforted. "You. Think. I. Care. About. Mangos!" He screamed and screamed. Spittle came out of his mouth. His mother continued to hold him. Eventually, his screams subsided to a loud sobbing. He became still, listening to his mother's soft voice. "Shhh, shhh, shhh," she said. "You're tired. Just tired."

Carlos closed his eyes. He lay in his mother's arms, exhausted.

He decided he could not tell her about the men in the restaurant. He would think up some excuse to prevent her from leaving the room. Perhaps he'd say he wasn't feeling well. He'd lie still and listless on the bed, listening to her low, soothing voice. He'd even force tears from his eyes, so many that they would stain the front of her dress. He'd find a way to hold her with him, there.

And then, in two days—it would only be as long as that, he was sure—his father would come and fetch them. He would wrap his arms around Carlos and say, "You've had an adventure. Wasn't it fun?"

- 0 -

RESIDENTS OF THE DEEP

For three months and twenty days, the *Cyclops* sailed to various ports across the Pacific. The crew spent time on both the north and south islands of New Zealand, then pushed on to Australia, stopping for a week in Townsville, on the Great Barrier Reef, before continuing up the coast. Finally, on the 18th of July, on a day when the sky was a lovely cobalt hue, streaked here and there with long, narrow strands of gray cloud, and with a gentle wind from the northeast blowing, I ordered my men to drop anchor at a spot that turned out to be almost directly on top of the City.

That day, the ocean surface was flat as a millpond. The water itself had a strange grayish cast that made it seem more mineral than liquid. As we waited for the anchor to settle below, I observed swarms of iridescent fish flickering about.

Is there anything as singularly impressive and affecting to the imagination as when, in a perfectly calm tropical sea, under a vertical sun, one is able to look down through a depth of thousands of fathoms of clear water and see on the ocean bottom glimpses of the City and all its strange and wonderful objects? The discovery of such a City existing under fathoms of ocean is an occurrence with no precedent in the annals of exploration, one that overshadows even the discovery of the Americas by Columbus.

The City exists underwater at a depth that approaches the elevation of the loftiest peak of the Himalayas, though no one has yet ascertained exactly how many fathoms with a string or sounding-line. The line must be extremely strong, and dropped into the sea with such a weight that it shall reach the bottom without being borne off by competing under-currents. The location is 184 nautical miles southwest of the island of New Guinea, just at the entrance to the strait between that island and the northeastern tip of the continent of Australia, which sailors the world over know as one of the busiest sea passages in the world.

Later, trying to describe the first time my gaze was able to pierce through fathoms of ocean water, I would say it was like looking at one of my mother's moss gardens. She kept them under glass of varying sizes. The bright green moss was interrupted here and there by dark pebbles and tendrils of colorful foliage. I believed I had never seen anything so beautiful until I discovered the City.

That first day, the crew labored over seven hours at the dredging equipment. Nothing appeared except for a quantity of light-colored, mud-like ooze. This ooze was found to contain a number of fragments of some hard mineral. My curiosity was aroused when Atkinson told me what microscopic analysis had revealed—the mud-like ooze had properties in common with *human*—and not animal—excreta. And the fragments showed uniformly angled edges—clear evidence, I thought, of human manipulation. As more and more of these fragments were dredged up and examined, it became clear that some of the pieces were interlocking, like the pieces of a gigantic jigsaw puzzle.

We went further and deeper with our measurements. And still we watched, as the City and all its treasures spread out before us— remaining just out of our reach. Finally, on the 4th of August, with the sounding-line stretched to the utmost, we hauled up a pillar approximately two feet in circumference and twelve feet in length, the surface of which was entirely covered with pictographs of a kind similar to those in the Temple of Amun in Egypt.

And that was when everything changed. I could see it already: Brodrick and Taylor and Lumley and Simon. Imagining the accolades, perhaps a band greeting us at the harbor at Doonhaven. Perhaps their own ships at last. And our Master, Owen Williams of Bronsea, what would he not give for such a treasure?

It would make a change for me as well.

Brodrick then said, with a finger pressed to one cheek—Brodrick was always a great one for going on—that if the writings of the philosopher Plato were to be believed, there had once been a great City that began life 2,000 years ago on the island of Santorini, in ancient Greece. Then, a great cataclysm caused the entire foundation to sink into the sea.

"Atlantis, you mean?" I said.

I did know this story. For centuries, we had been hearing tales of a City on the ocean floor, one populated by people half-god and half-human. The City was sometimes located in the Mediterranean, at other times off the coast of Spain. It had become nearly impossible to untangle truth from fact until now.

Over dinner that night, I cautioned the others that the imagination, in this as in many other cases, sometimes resulted in a distortion of reality. "Furthermore," I added, "whatever we find belongs in a museum." They seemed to grow surly at my words.

As soon as I could, I escaped to the deck, and remained a long while looking at the water. Were there indeed people down there? How many centuries had they spent observing the passage of our surface vessels, passing like ghosts over the water? Had they, too, tried to imagine *us*? How curious to think that no one before us had thought of the simple act of looking down.

What had those residents of the deep made of our faces, eyes full of curiosity, looking down at them? My own face was the face of a man no longer young. The sea had kept me away from family and friends for many years. Yet, I mused, I had been willing to perform this sacrifice, all in the hope of experiencing that one moment when the depths would be illuminated, as when a room's lamplit interior is spied through a window. Over the decades, stubbornness and persistence had become the two main elements of my character. Who knew the greatest discovery I would ever make would involve so simple an act as peering down?

Of the City and its inhabitants, we still know very little. We still do not know whether, for example, the City dwellers are divided into classes of rich and poor, or into different races, or whether they have great universities resembling Oxford and Cambridge—centers of learning where new generations can be schooled in the wonders of mathematics and science.

It lies beneath a translucent, greenish dome. The walls, the inhabitants' clothing, even their countenances have a greenish cast. A breeze might ruffle the surface of the ocean and for a moment one can see—or imagine one can see—a corresponding ripple in the green dome below. Almost, a tearing. I would hold my breath, gripped with anxiety, imagining the worst. But, in the end, my fears proved misplaced: nothing disturbed the tranquility of the City or of its inhabitants.

As far as I could tell, the residents of the City resembled ourselves: they possessed two eyes, two ears, a nose, hair, a mouth, and so forth. They, in all likelihood, possessed limbs, for despite the fact that their physical forms were always modestly concealed beneath a kind of shiny material, they seemed to get from place to place by walking. And walking, as we know, is only managed with legs.

I noticed something perplexing about the under-dwellers' manner of locomotion, for they seemed only to move in a forward direction. I had never, not once, observed anyone move in reverse. Perhaps there was a law requiring them to do so? Toward what purpose? Their steps always followed a fixed orbit, from which not a single person deviated. They appeared to be circling, endlessly circling, rather in the manner by which the moon circled the earth, drawn by magnets, perhaps, or water currents.

I thought of my own city of Doonhaven—all the various arteries of roads crisscrossing the landscape, all the density of human and vehicular traffic. I imagined the underwater City was no different. For the need for quick transportation—the simple human need to move from one place to another—must have been acknowledged eons ago.

Perhaps, I told myself, I should not think of roads as one does, as constructions over a flat surface. Perhaps their conduits were vertical, like the chutes and elevators one finds in factories or other city buildings. How lofty must be their cities, how wonderful their flora and fauna, how altogether astonishing to the mind and heart!

Once, after peering down for what seemed like hours, I thought I caught a glimpse of a very young woman who reminded me, with a pang, of my own daughter, Wilhelmina. Wilhelmina! I could see her pale face, her tears when I informed her I would be leaving on my next voyage.

The woman below had lovely, long, red hair that streamed gently behind her, held aloft by the ocean currents. Her eyes, set in a pale green face, were limpid and large, an intense black. Around her neck was a string of large, white pearls alternating with bright red stones that resembled rubies. As to the rest—her clothing was minimal, perhaps so as not to impede movement: only a simple tunic, over a narrow skirt that stretched to her ankles.

Six months prior, Wilhelmina, whose mother had died when she was scarcely 10, departed for Singapore with her new husband. It grieved me, this move of my only child to a far-away Asiatic city. Even though my time at sea had outweighed my time on land, Wilhelmina and I had been close. When I was on land, I rarely accepted social engagements, desiring only to spend as much time as I could in my home. It could hardly be surprising, then, that my attention was caught by a woman who seemed similar in age to my own daughter.

The woman beneath the water, while never breaking the pace of her walk, now stretched her lovely arms upward towards me, as if in supplication. Unable to think, unable even to breathe, I waited to see what else she might do.

Slowly, she reached one arm to the back of her neck, pulled off her necklace, then held it up towards me. Her lips moved. Naturally, all sound was impeded by many fathoms of ocean, but I could see that her lips formed words that had no correspondence with English or with any other language on the surface of this Earth. Had I been more courageous, I would have pitched myself over the side in an effort to close the distance between myself and this stranger.

Who was this woman? What could she possibly need? I ached to know. Somehow, she had perceived me. In our perceiving of each other, she had confirmed my existence, as I had hers.

Before I could react, the woman was gone. Though I spent the subsequent days peering with eyes that positively ached with the effort at fathoms of ocean, I never saw the woman again. She was lost among that mass of endlessly circling people, who never gave the slightest acknowledgment that they knew they were being observed.

Weeks passed. The weather remained tranquil, and the *Cyclops* remained anchored to the spot. Such good fortune was unprecedented, to say the least. I could not shake the feeling that we were being held in place, could not help feeling that the City's inhabitants, though not desiring to communicate, did not wish us to go just yet.

I knew that, in this part of the world, the gales and rain of the monsoon would not be long in coming. I became conscious of a corresponding ripple of anxiety among the crew. Not all were like myself, thirsty for adventure. Most were in it only for the chance to put some food in their families' bellies. In the minds of the men were memories of meadows and hills, soft air and blue skies, the gentle landscape of the country of their birth.

Several times, the men drew up the line too fast, and the winches groaned as if they might snap in two. It was strange, but after the raising of the column, no further treasure came to us. Brodrick, who of all of us had seemed the most keen to introduce the riches of the City to the world, could barely contain his frustration.

As I was standing on the deck one day, supervising the dredges, a cloud came across the sun, a spot of rain fell on my head, and without warning we found ourselves in the middle of a tremendous gale. I ordered the men to secure the hatches, and hastily they set to. For almost a week, we were at the mercy of the waves, and we lost two good men. After, when the weather cleared, the ocean depths were murky. It was then we realized how far away we were from home.

When the crew had recovered sufficiently from their exertions, I ordered the ship to turn for home. "Not in our time, not in our children's time, then," Brodrick said. "Perhaps," I told him, "in a hundred years, it will be possible." He turned his back on me in disgust.

In matters regarding right, or wrong, I am fully persuaded that I have chosen right, no matter the difficulty of such a choice. I was saving the lives of my men, or so I told myself. Moreover, I had signed a contract with the line, the contract had laid out the terms of my employment. I was morally bound to fulfill them.

When we put in again at Doonhaven, a stranger was standing in the harbor, waiting. He was tall and bent and leant heavily upon a stick. He was around sixty years of age, with light blue eyes and a deeply tanned face. "Good afternoon, John," he said to me. "You seem to have been on an adventure. I wonder how you managed it."

"An adventure, aye," I said. "But tramping hills and roads will serve me well enough for now."

"What do you know of this underwater City?" the man asked.

I felt a reluctance, even a repulsion, at his words. "Perhaps the fairies told me about it," I said.

The man smiled and scratched his white hair with the end of his stick. It was then that Broderick came up beside me. "There's no harm in anyone knowing now, Captain," he said.

I became stiff with anger. "You only seek to profit from it," I said.

"We shall see," Broderick said. And with that, we parted ways.

Some months later, I heard that the *Cyclops* had set out again, Broderick at the helm. I heard it proceeded up the sun-struck west African coast and was attacked once or twice by pirates. Eventually, the Cyclops made port in Cape Town. And then, it simply vanished. None of the crew, not Broderick or Kent or Mooney or Atkinson, were ever seen or heard from again. The next year, the bent man came to visit me in my home. I had been expecting him.

"May we trouble you for another voyage?" the man asked. At my response, the smile disappeared from the man's face and he said, "Ah, you can laugh, you with your Trinity education and your reading and your grand and progressive ways." Then, when he had exhausted all his rhetoric, he climbed back into his chaise.

I sailed again, but never for Mr. Owen Williams of Bronsea. At each port, I invariably found a letter from Wilhelmina. Again and again, she beseeched me to have a care—nay, to abandon my quest altogether. But I had too much ambition, and moreover I had made promises to my men that I could not renege from.

Wilhelmina accused me of fancying myself a modern Livingstone. In the course of penetrating the African interior, the explorer had crossed numerous rivers and new river systems, identifying distinctive geographic features. Starting from Zanzibar and proceeding westwards, Livingstone found a new geography: mountains and rivers no one like us had beheld before. He made discovery of Lake Tanganyika, and many other places, and enabled the expansion of the Empire. I was not of the same bent.

"I shall pay well for honest work," I told my men. And they believed me and followed me.

I told them that there was a City underneath the ocean. I described the contours of its landscape and the aspects of its existence. I told my men that there, on the ocean bottom, there were plains and mountains and plateaus, mirror images of our own. I described the vegetation, the undulating forests of kelp, the magnificence of the City's architecture. I described, in detail, the City's strange inhabitants and their unusual method of locomotion.

Wilhelmina is 39 now. The world, she writes, is so very different: there is so much more misery. She can scarce believe my stories of how, in Africa, hundreds of slaves stand in chains by the auction houses. I tell her how men of different religions look upon each other with suspicion. I tell her I despise nothing more than men who justify violence for the sake of their gods. I tell her that joy has become increasingly scant in our society. She wrote back, months later: "And whose fault is that?"

I reflect on my many voyages. What had all this been for, if not for a better future? Ah, I thought, if I could have found the

City, I would have written a book, and I would have been delighted to share my discovery with the world.

I am, as Wilhelmina knows, a man living in the past. But I do not now work for a Master, and never shall again.

The image of the City remains fixed in my memories: powerful and intractable, mysterious and graceful, glorious.

Years earlier, an old sea captain had told me that a seaman's mission was to be the eyes and ears of those who could not or would not venture forth, and that if I was truly meant for a career on the sea, I would know because I would never cease to look for things in the water.

I often think on this conversation. It took place on a ship's bridge. The sea at that time was coated with black—a kind of slick, viscous oil. Oil poured forth all the greatest ships of those days, it was nothing special. It bubbled and seethed, reminding me that there had been a ship capsized on that very spot, not long ago.

I gestured vaguely towards the water.

The old captain took note of his movement. "Ah!" he said. And that was all.

Setting off on a journey must be a little like launching off a cliff. The sensation of leaving the earth, the lightness as one catapults through air, is incomparable. And then the inevitable downward pull, the plunging into the ocean depths: frigidly cold, menacing, all-embracing. To each jump I find myself giving the same answer: yes.

I still dream about the *Cyclops*. In my dreams, I feel the rolling of the waves as they rock the hull. The day is bright. I pass multitudes of islands on either side, islands of all shapes and sizes.

Inevitably, I know it is time to turn back to shore. A melancholy settles over my dream self. I do not wish to return to land, but in my dream, I am not given a choice.

Gradually, the ship begins running out of deep water. I begin to panic. Then I awake, feeling as though I have narrowly avoided some disaster.

My house sits on top of a hill. A little beyond the harbor of Doonhaven is Doon Island, with the grey castle of Clonmere, standing at the entrance to the bay like a faithful sentinel guarding the waters. Every day I take my chaise down the hill and into town, passing the harbor, scattering geese near the marketplace.

One day, as I happened to be passing the Post Office and the chemist's, I was overtaken by a feeling of disappointment so profound it seemed to cleave my chest in two. The gate to the widow Donovan's stood open, as it frequently did. It had always been my inclination to stop in and exchange pleasantries with her, if for no other purpose than to feel human companionship.

But I pass on. I never stop, driven yet by the vision of some bright and imaginable future, waiting there for me beneath the waves.

– 0 –

THING

That one's name is Plankton, and this one is Shrimp. The captain's name is Caesar. The Captain's name is a real name, the only real name among us.

My name is Darkness. That's because of the color of my skin. Or maybe it's because I was born in the year when the nights became longer, the year the electricity disappeared. The year the air turned brown and heavy, and the sun dipped closer to us. When we forgot about almost everything, except how to survive.

Caesar says he thinks I should have been called Angel. "What's an angel," I ask. "A beautiful creature with wings," he says. I can't imagine it.

"Like birds?" I ask.

"Yes," Caesar says.

Our house is made out of earth and water. Caesar taught us how.

There is never any change in the weather.

I sometimes forget what green looks like.

The four of us are in charge of the Mutant Pig Zoo: we feed the animals, clean their pens, that kind of thing. Our pigs are the results of experiments. They have all kinds of weird traits: one's mouth was in the middle of its forehead. Another had six legs. Another stared skyward, unable to bend its neck. Still another had the body of a snake and three noses. Each of the Not-Rights was unique and completely different from the others.

The mouth-in-the-forehead pig was mine. I named it Ed. I remembered that name from somewhere, I'm not sure where. When it cried, white foam spilled out of its mouth; the red of its pupils was astonishing, like fire. I never got tired of looking at it. It lasted longer than the others, I even let myself hope that it would happen differently. But one day its bristles started to fall out—big black clumps of them, all over the pen. After that, it was just days.

But why should a pig cry, Shrimp said. What gives it the right?

We pig tenders go about our work with cowls pulled forward, shielding our faces. The sun is too bright: it scalds everything. At least, with a cowl, we still have faces.

Caesar's cowl is always pulled forward, so I'm not really sure what he looks like. He has a problem with runny eyes, a side effect of the atmosphere, dry as dust. Every so often, he stops and wipes his cheeks.

Caesar sometimes tells stories, late at night, if we can't sleep. He is old enough to remember a time when there were factories and pigs were processed night and day, when the smell of pig blood lingered over everything. He remembers a time when people ate every part of the pigs: ears, eyes, even entrails. Pork fat was used in cakes, and in bread. I try and imagine what a cake is. Caesar has to draw.

"We're lucky. Our pigs don't smell bad," Caesar says.

The factories still cry out sometimes. When we hear the keening sound, we know it is herds of ghost pigs, running into walls and crying because they can never find their way out. They are inside people's heads, like the memories of old ways. And when people's heads get too full of memories, the first ones to tumble out are the pigs, running every which way and squealing.

The pigs are bred for research. The Founding Fathers have found a way to breed out the pig odor. When the occasional mutant appears, no one in the City can stand to look. There's an abhorrence, a repulsion about things that are not physically perfect. Everyone in the City walks upright, everyone is physically symmetrical: two arms, two legs, two ears, two eyes, two hands, two lungs.

No one knows why, when a Not-Right pig is born, the Founding Fathers don't kill it immediately. Caesar says that would have been the best solution. Instead, the Founding Fathers send the Not-Rights far away, to us. Caesar says we should be proud that we have been chosen.

There's another reason the piggery is hundreds of miles from the City. It's not only the mutant pigs that repel, it's us, the Pig Keepers.

I have no legs. They say my mother was very young, practically a child herself. My father was also her father, or something terrible. I can walk because the doctors took pity on me and made me legs. They are the color of gun-metal. They flash in the sun. I never tire of looking at them.

Plankton doesn't have any lips, all he has are gums and teeth. You don't realize how much the lack of lips ruins a face until you've seen Plankton.

Shrimp has only one eye. The hollow where the other eye should have been is covered with shiny green scales. Shrimp likes to say that his mother ate a lot of fish when she was carrying him in her belly. She wouldn't listen when people told her that the appetite for fish would result in a baby who looked like a fish. It's a proven fact.

I never knew either of my parents. I lived in a laboratory on the 3rd floor of Loadstar IV, along with Plankton and Shrimp, for almost 12 years. In the beginning, there were more than 20 of us. We all had to begin each day by reciting the Five Precepts. Now, I can only remember the second:

Once you've flown past the summit of your fears, nothing will seem impossible.

There were many things we didn't know: we didn't know cold, we didn't know weather, we didn't know what was beyond the long hallway, each end of which was barred by heavy steel doors.

Caesar came one day and collected the three of us. The rest—and there were still about 10 others—who knows what happened to them? Who knows why he chose me and Plankton and Shrimp? I remember that the three of us—me and Plankton and Shrimp—wept in Caesar's truck. We were afraid of Caesar. We didn't know where we were going. We thought we were going to a warehouse, one of the dozens that line the perimeter of the city. Instead, we came here.

We become attached to our mutants, we can't help it. Shrimp has even begun to record the dates of their deaths, scratching with a sharp grey stone on the gate to the pens. The pigs don't live very long after they come to us. None of them ever lasts longer than a year. One died after just a month. The food, perhaps.

Do pigs feel despair?

"How long do we have, Caesar?" I asked one day.

Caesar didn't answer right away.

"How long?" I said again. "I know, we're not normal. We're like *them*."

"We have enough," Caesar said. "Stop talking. My head aches."

Another time, I asked, "Will we explode, Caesar?"

"Why?" he said. "Why do you think that?"

"I used to hear them say—at the lab—*antimatter*. They would say that word, and I would feel cold. What does it mean?

"It means," Caesar said, "we are at the edge. We *were* at the edge. We are stable now. We have balanced the forces."

I breathed deeply. Caesar sighed.

The one that died fastest had two heads. Its heart was outside its body, pulsing just above its navel. We didn't find it until it had been dead for a few hours. I immediately suspected Plankton because, that morning, when he came in for breakfast, there was blood on his boots. And there was something different about his face. A look.

When we found the two-headed pig, Shrimp curled up over it and howled. We were very afraid, not of the things outside waiting to kill us, but of the cruelty we saw in each other.

In time, Caesar says, everything will vanish. We'll become molecules, spinning in the infinity of space.

Caesar has been to school. I can tell, from the words he uses. I want to ask, What is a molecule? What is infinity? What is space? How did Caesar learn?

One day, they sent us a new creature. It came in the back of a truck, locked in a steel cage. The driver was new. We asked him what had happened to the old driver, Aiken. Aiken sometimes brought us things from the City. Not this man. He shrugged and turned his head away but not before we saw the look of disgust on his face. We didn't speak to him further.

I was angry. It would have been nice to have something from the Far Away, some small thing. Food, news, anything.

The creature's skin was a strange color: yellow, with very faint grey stripes. We had heard that there were two or three of these strangelings born every year, but we had never actually seen one until now.

Caesar told us that when people defied Code 4911, they didn't realize that the chances of having a deformed baby increased by almost 50%. In the long-ago time, things happened randomly. Many deformed children were born. The State supported these, for many hundreds of years. In our lifetimes, however, the Rule of Compassion was stricken from the Commandments. This happened at the last Gathering, the one in 2560.

The face of the child was normal in every aspect.

"Something went wrong at Quest," said Shrimp. "Who knows?"

Shrimp's favorite expression is "Who knows."

I was covered in mud and pig crap when the creature arrived. I looked and saw a cloud of dust barreling down the road. I wiped my hands, let go of the shovel, and ran.

Caesar was there first. He ran up to the cage, ahead of any of us. When Plankton moved forward, Caesar gestured for him to stay back. There was warning and steel in his eyes. Plankton stayed back. His cheeks became mottled, a dark red that spread slowly towards his throat.

The three of us waited, stamping our feet from the cold.

Caesar lifted the creature out of its cage, gently. The creature's eyes were wide with terror. Finally, it opened its mouth. All that came out was a bleat. We all stood frozen in shock. If we had not heard it with our own ears, we would have thought it was a pig making those sounds.

The creature flailed its arms. Caesar's face had long red scratches. "It was supposed to be sedated," we heard him say. "Stupid."

Caesar was strong and tall, but he was no match for the creature's terror, which seemed to give it superhuman strength. Our other pigs began to gather restlessly by the fences. A feeling of foreboding settled over us.

"Kill it, Caesar, kill it!" Plankton shouted.

"No!" Caesar managed, through gritted teeth. "Shut up!" He delivered a blow to the creature's head. Not a very hard blow, I could tell he was holding back, but the creature's head immediately bobbled, so slack in Caesar's arms that I thought its neck was broken.

"You killed it, Caesar!" I said. "Were you supposed to do that?"

"I didn't kill it," Caesar said. "It would take a lot more than that."

"You mean to say——?" Shrimp said.

"I mean to say," Caesar said.

"Why us?" I wailed. "Why *here?*"

"Were we bad?" Shrimp asked.

"No," Caesar said.

"Will they take us away?" I asked.

Caesar shook his head. "No," he said.

We made a little nest for Thing, just outside the kitchen door. The next day, as I was frying our breakfast of eggs and bacon, its eyes opened, and its mouth became round and pleading. Its legs were thin, like twigs. It had no shoes.

It's been a week. The creature is still alive. I have been thinking a lot about it, watching it every day, seeing how it changes.

For instance, it no longer reacts when I poke it with the tip of my knife. Little dots of blood appear on the surface of its skin. Perhaps it has no nerve endings?

I made a list of my observations. So far, I have six:

It has no name. We call it Thing.

Is Thing human? The questions must be asked. If human, it should have the privileges of a human. But if not human, then hurting it is not an immoral act.

It can endure any amount of pressure applied to its head or throat. Its only response is a slight, very slight, widening of the eyes. We increase the pressure gradually and are always careful to mark bruises and so forth that appear on Thing.

It has hair all over its back, but none anywhere else. The hair is downy and soft, like the fuzz of a baby chick. This is Shrimp's comparison. I've never seen a baby chick. I think I grew up in a city, though I have no memory of what city it was. Caesar says it doesn't matter what city, there's only one now. And that's the one where all of us are from.

This creature was sent to us for a reason. What that is, we don't know. Caesar says it is possible we will never know. But it seems clear that the Founding Fathers are grateful to us for assuming responsibility for Thing. Our food rations have doubled since the creature's arrival. (That's so that we will not be tempted to eat it.)

It has two arms and two legs but cannot walk.

It is like I was, in the beginning.

I showed the list to Caesar. He looked at it for a long time. Finally, he handed it back to me. "Very good," he said.

"How long will it take Thing to die?" I ask Caesar. He shrugs. The look on his face scares me.

"It will die, though," I say. "That's what it's supposed to do, right?"

"Right," he says, again with that look on his face. "Just keep watching it. You're still feeding it?"

I said, "Of course!"

I don't like to see creatures starve. I'm not like Plankton. He was born cruel. He has never left our pigs alone. They walk around with wounds. One day, so long ago I think I might have dreamed it, I saw Plankton standing at the far edge of the pig pen. He was screaming at something. His whole body went up, down, up, down. As I got closer, I saw that he was stomping one of the pigs. He would yell: "What (stomp) *are* you (stomp)?" The pig was nothing. It had disappeared. All that was left was a pile of blood, dark blood, almost purple. A lot of it had gotten on Plankton's boots. The smell in the air was deep and rich, like no other smell out here.

Where was Caesar? I was afraid. Finally, Plankton saw me and stopped. He turned. He was still able to feel shame, then.

I warn Plankton to keep away from Thing. "Why," Plankton whines. His pale eyes have no light in them at all. It's like looking at stones.

We couldn't send Plankton away, could we? Sometimes, I was afraid. No, not about anything he might do to me, but for what he might do to the others.

Caesar said no, we couldn't send Plankton away. We were all four supposed to remain together, we were a family. The way Caesar said it, pausing just before and just after he said "family," I knew he meant it as a warning.

There is a river running right next to the pig pens. This river has no name, so we named it No Name River. "It is ours now," Caesar says, "because we named it."

"How can you own a river," I asked Caesar. "If you own something, you have to be able to keep it sometimes, just for yourself."

"No," Caesar said. "That's not what owning something is." I looked closely at him and realized something was wrong with him. Was it his eyes? Was it the tremor in his voice? I sense things. I always have.

Thing senses it, too. It hates when Caesar approaches. That is the only time I have seen Thing shake.

"Caesar," I said. "You're not thinking of leaving—?"

"Not unless they make me," he said. He was smiling.

Then I started wondering if Thing was supposed to be his replacement. This made me angry. Why were things never clear? By ourselves out here, we were always guessing. The Founding Fathers want this, the Founding Fathers want that. Such a waste of time.

Thing can't be Caesar's replacement because Thing is just – a Thing. It has no intelligence at all. It is simply a bundle of intuitive responses.

It can't even speak. No, Thing can't be Caesar's replacement.

Or maybe Thing is meant to replace one of us. Maybe word has gotten back to the City about Plankton. How three of the mutant pigs died because of his cruelty. Maybe Plankton will disappear someday. He should.

"What year is this, Caesar?" I asked.

"Listen to me!" Caesar almost shouted. "Bad news . . ."

"Snow?"

"No."

People change. We live and die. The planet is dying.

Death is here, too.

Plankton woke me one morning. Look, he kept saying, over and over.

I knew. I didn't have to look. I knew because there was a feeling I had, that the world had gone. That where Caesar had been was now empty space.

There was the thing on the ground, that-which-was-no-longer-Caesar, and with each passing day the thing or whatever it was got stiffer and the robes lifted up as if something inside were pushing. We all sat and tried to remember when the next scheduled delivery was.

Caesar liked to say that we are all merely instruments. I think that's true. We don't even know how to kiss, though I have touched Caesar's lips when he is sleeping. I wanted to let him know that I was grateful.

We wait, now. We wait for Caesar's body to disappear. Organs, flesh, bone, these will melt away.

I can't look, after. I want to blot it out.

The most important thing is order.

Shrimp cries. Gone, gone, gone!

"Death," Plankton says.

I'm cold.

"Stone," Plankton says. "Stone on stone on stone." He is almost chanting.

"Wake up, Caesar," I shriek. "Wake up!"

Thing is scratching at the door. It is hungry. So are we.

Plankton takes the shovel from behind the stove. Shrimp stands next to me, trembling.

"Sacred!" he says. "Our Caesar!"

I feel the darkness coming toward us. I look up and wait, the way Caesar taught me to do.

"I remember, Caesar," I say. It isn't until I see Plankton turn and Shrimp stop crying that I realize I've spoken out loud. "The world will rise again. It will rise again."

- 0 -

SPORES

K thinks the boss is in love with her.

She looks like a mosaic puffball, her skin covered with checkered patterns.

The boss was born Earthstar. He'd never look her way. His spores were meant to go else: to a Silverleaf. Or a Shag. Not K that smelled like wet rot. All scaly cap and throat gills. She belonged with other Common.

Varnish and varnish. I'll say this for K: she is tenacious. Especially about her delusions.

"Me mum's a thick," she said once. "A focking thick."

"Hmmm," I said.

"She a root rotter," K said.

"Hit brew and all?" I asked.

"12 pints one go. Honest," K said.

K silent the rest of the day.

I was weary of K. We had the worst job: growing giant polyphores, thousands and thousands of them, in little paper fans studded with 4-micron ova. The fans burned our fingers. Burned like sulfur. We had to wait hours for the new skin to grow back. Fingers never felt the same, after.

We couldn't leave the room until Growing was over. That meant days. We were the slowest team in the whole White Zone, the boss said. Probably even the slowest in the whole planet.

You may find yourself living in a shotgun shack. Where those words came from, I don't precisely know.

"We be needing foxes," I said once.

"You lousy hedgehog," the boss said, giving me a good one. My right eye swelled up almost immediately.

"You not be asking me to fetch, you lousy Common!" He gave me another good one on the way out.

K trembling there in the corner.

"Here," she said finally, pulling something yellow, bell-shaped, out of her pocket.

I shook my head.

"You sure?" she said. "I got these fresh."

Hours go by. Then K says, "He's a stump, that one. Jesus."

Me standing up straight, trying to forget the pain in my right cheek. "I don't think we're at liberty to discuss," I say.

K's eyes well up. Copious.

"Shut it," I say. I don't want to hear another word. Sighs and pity, I don't need. Especially her sighs and pity. "I won't ever look as good as I do now."

K begins to laugh. Then she sees my face. Her right hand claps over her mouth. "Oh." I want to cuff her.

"You might be wanting a piss soon," she says. "Then, if blood comes out of you . . ."

"You'll be wanting to feel my fist," I say.

"Oh," she says again. But this time, she looks sad. She says, strange-voiced, "I'll bring oak milk tomorrow. Might help."

When my friend Summer lay under the beechwood seems a lifetime ago, puking insides, puking until her stomach was a strange convex shape, what happened was, I heard a whooshing noise, and then from the other side of the trees came a Sand Spirit. Drumbeat Ta-ra! It came down from the sky, propellers whirring, dredging hay and thistles. Then snapped her right up.

As they used to say in Marble Arch, when some play was on: The Lady Exits.

For a long time after, I stayed under the beech, whispering Summer, whatya reckon to all this and watching two yella bitterns wing from branch to branch to branch. Until the shadows chased me home.

In P-1, the teachers tell, Heaven is up a winding stair. Hell is like falling off the Whitecliffs—down and down and down and down. Limbo is—somewhere between. Those lessons always gave me the frights.

Now K making delicate noises over there on her side of the table.

"The fuck is this—?" I exclaim. My fingers are snagged on a Changeable. "How did these get in with the others?"

K stops. Looks guilty. Bends her head to have a closer look at what I have in my right hand. "Oh," she says. And starts to hum. Even though her voice is low, I think I hear her say "lash" and "blood." She swats the Changeables out of my hand as if they were nothing. "Leave them," she says. Against the white-tiled floor, they look dove-colored. "I'll take care of them later." She notices me gaping. "Seriously," she says. "I'll take care of them."

I'm shaking. She isn't afraid. Of him. She looks at me again. "I know, R. I know."

"What the fuck is wrong with you—" I say.

"Come on," she says. "I'm mad. Mum says I could drive anyone to . . . well, you know."

K has very quick hands, I must say. I hate those slimy Changeables. They're rascally, which means they're quick to mutate and almost impossible to spot. If only three or four of them had gotten through—Oh, they come after ya.

My jaw starts to ache, as if the boss had just landed another good one. But now he never has to, and he knows it. Trembling at just the memory.

K nonchalantly scoops the Changeables up from the floor, with her bare hands. I've never seen anyone do that before. She really must be crazes.

Her fingers are an angry, violent red. They must hurt terribly. Either that, or something has killed off her nerve endings. Or she just wants to die.

She nudges the door to the ovens with her left boot. The door slides back with a rusty groan. The fire is hungry and seems to lap out at her.

"Watch out—" I say.

But by the time I get the words out, she's dumped the Changeables into the oven and slammed the door shut again. This whole time, I've stood rooted to the same spot.

"Hello?" K says, snapping her fingers. Then points to the table. "Shouldn't you be arranging those Poriales? Into brackets?" She adds, for good measure, "You lousy Common!"

I finally smile, though feels like my face is breaking.

Humans are a small and fragile species. But we have the distinction of breeding almost as quickly as microbes. Sex is soporific and palliative. No one would attach a pejorative such as "meaningless" to any form of sexual activity. We're all encouraged to do it as much as possible, as late as possible. Grandmothers in their 60s do it, as well as children as young as 11 or 12. It's considered a patriotic activity. The rate's been dropping over the past few decades, though, which is why there's so much emphasis now on breeding and genetics.

Once a female gets pregnant, her food rations are tripled. She can't have liquor, but any other loblolly she craves gets delivered on a plate. The message is she's special now.

Whereas, it's grim for the ones who haven't borne. Stood up, 19 hours, on the pylon, and—have a go, anyone who has spore stiff.

That's what happened to K's mum. She gone mind-bent. K the result. K who believes in love. To the best of my knowledge, love's a result of a pill or a drug, or an amphetamine. So it can't be real. Anything produced by a pill can't be love, it can't be real.

K. Only 12, she let herself be used by a lout. Days by, no K. Her mum came knocking on my door: Seen K? I was worried. Thought I caught a glimpse of her long dark hair, there at the edge of the lake. She been lying there, face down, probably most of the night.

Shite! Shite! Fock! Shite! Fockers!

She still alive, though. Lout threatened her with a knife. You've no idea, no idea. Blackened both her eyes. Top all bare.

"K!" I cried. "K!"

I didn't know what to do. I hated her so much in that moment.

She got transferred else, where I don't know.

New partner now in the lab. She makes no sense, but what's gone through is gone. Sure, me and my family will starve. The thought only bothers me when I think about it too long. I try not to mess around with those kinds of thinks.

"I've been," L says. "Been and done."

"It's only fair," I say, with no care.

L knows what happened to K. "Poor wee bitch," she said, once.

I couldn't face it. "You about done?" I said. "With the new ones?"

"What you blathering 'bout," L said. "You a Ruddy Common, just like me. And she. We all be dead in a drawer, like."

Fuck all. The truth: K showed which of us had the more courage. Common or no, she was a Single. Never another one like her.

Slow is time. No watches allowed. Done when we're done.

"Pheeew!" L says. "These fockers stink." She wrinkles her nose. "Swear I don't know how you—"

"Don't you go off again," I say, gritting teeth.

L begins to sing: "In Dub, Dub, Dub, the streets, streets, streets, in Dub, Dub, Dub—"

"Shit," I say. "You no voice."

L glares. "Jesus!" she cries. "Long live motherfockers like youse."

"And why that song? Of all the bloody—"

"Stuff it, R," L says. "Wonder who had the crazes to marry youse. Boring as a carwash. Fock. Take a pill."

Excellent advice: I finally take a pill. Pray when I take it, too. First time in years. Better than having it snipped.

– 0 –

FIRST LIFE

Ku Ling's Rule: First life began in the Dome.

Nervous? Her asked.

I nodded. Ever since they moved our colony from Tonle Sap to the Philippines, my mind hasn't been the same.

Her repeats, slowly, The assignment is to make a determination on the suitability of Subject A for rehabilitation, utilizing Ku Ling's Rule as the theoretical framework. Nothing more nor less.

I repeat, Nothing more nor less.

That's right, Her nods.

The first corollary: what is average is perfect.

Today I'm thick or something because thoughts are dark as dark.

I can hear Big arguing. He sits on Her's other side. He's telling Drinker, the formlessness. That's what I mean. That's what I'm trying to focus on.

Drinker says, But. But.

Big says, To conduct regression analyses. Big says, Hypothetically speaking. For the sake of comparison.

Her has learned not to pay Big any mind. She winks at me.

Drinker says, Negative outcomes. (Question: How did Big ever make it to Academy? Slow as slow.)

Sunlight and glass, Prisms and mirrors. My mind is floating out there, beyond the windows. Out there, where swish, swish goes something, maybe the wind.

Drinker says, That's the problem, right there. Hello? Dragon? Hey, Dragon?

Her says, Signs indicate . . .

Big says, No! No intervention!

Her shrinks back in the seat. Hesitates. But still manages, You think—?

Muddiness, I say. It's all muddiness. Extinction. I rise slowly from my seat. Go, go, go.

Her puts a hand on my arm. The look on Her's face. I've seen it before.

Those S pills will kill you, Big says, and snorts.

Hedonism, Drinker says.

Her has had enough. She yells, Leave Dragon alone!

Fire Lizard paces at the front of the room. Test is 20 minutes, tops. I'm concerned. I'm sweating.

I can only see part of Her's back. Next to her, Big's broad shoulders.

Big reminds me of a creature from long ago. Those flapping things. Those what you call harbingers.

Fire Lizard points his laser eyes in my direction. What's the matter, Dragon? he says. No translation available. This is a test.

Big snickers.

Opaque, I mutter. Very opaque.

They should put something over the windows. Refraction is a bother. My eyes are weaker the past year. Light's fading. Sun's dying. Planet's dying. We're all dying. Everything dying. No one's come up with a plan.

Twilight. Snow starts. I still don't have a solution. I tell the snow, Go ahead, seal us in. Soon as class ends, we'll all scurry back to our holes. Who cares?

Yesu, for some soup. Hot and sour.

Focus! *Autonomous morality, not conformity. The X for Morality and suppression of the antagonistic impulse.*

Was the sampling sufficient?

Was sufficient allowance made for—?

The evidence. Where is the evidence?

Voluminous this morning, but now vanished.

The paper is an ambush. It steals my words the minute I set them down.

Her whispers, The evidence, Dragon. The evidence.

Her adds, Don't look for it under your chair, fuck.

Silence! Fire Lizard screams. His green eyes glow. Actually glow. Probably from the Strontium 90.

I shrug, Her continues with her whispering. Voluminous, Her says. The prototypical leader can only emerge from within a homogeneous group. Results suggest—

What?

Tether your thoughts, man, Big says.

When Fire Lizard claps his hands, I'm so startled I almost jump out of my chair. That's it. Our screens begin rising from our desks. A dozen slowly begin wafting towards the front, where the fire lines are.

Over, over, over. Test over. There goes my screen. Into the black Machine right next to Fire Lizard. Him glowing red and orange in the meanwhile. Grades released in 15.

Drinker turns and says, with one raised eyebrow, I didn't get that about predictive qualities? Were we supposed to factor in cultural explanations?

No, I stammer. I mean, Yes.

Big, scoffing: The subject's heightened sensitivity to experimental pain—that wasn't even covered.

It was, Her said. You just weren't paying attention.

Quick as quick, Big has her braid in his fist.

Gentlemen! Fire Lizard yells. Desist, please, gentlemen! But his yellow eyes are way over there, and Big has already banged Her's head into her desk.

Drinker rejoins, raising his hand, concurrently, as well as prospectively.

Stop! Fire Lizard bellows. Now, he means it. Silver rays come shooting out of his ears.

The intentionality of violence, I say. Her is just trying to explain.

That's right. Oppositional exchange, that's what I'm talking about, Drinker says, making slashing motions with his hands.

That is consistent, Fire Lizard says, nodding his head thoughtfully. Now put Her down gently. There. I hope you haven't broken Her's neck.

Big holds up both hands, palms towards Fire Lizard. No, sir. No!

Spare me the psychological constructs, Fire Lizard says.

Her still hasn't moved.

I moan. I moan and moan and moan.

What is it, Dragon, Fire Lizard says. Speak up!

Need to call a neurologist, I manage.

Get a hold of yourself, Dragon, Fire Lizard snaps.

Check brain function, I insist. Still time.

Drinker places a rough hand on the top of Her's head. Is there a pulse there? Because I can't, I can't—

Fire Lizard is at the end of his patience. You, he says, pointing straight at me. Out. I won't have that kind of behavior here. Not in my class.

I stumble out to the corridor, I hear Fire Lizard say, This examination of the fifth dimension—

What is it all for, sir, Big says.

The epitome of the average, Fire Lizard says.

I'm exhausted by these verbal tussles. Every day, the same.

Where is Her? Speak, Her!

Her gradient of optical opioid receptors declared non-functional. All interpretable data wiped from her cells. Extracted, that's how they call it.

Where was the Todkill Scale when Her needed it? Her believed in crucifixes and such. Stuff from old times. Her always talking about holy orders. Her nowhere now. Or maybe just hiding out. In some forest. Some thicket. Like her father before.

All a function of computational semantics. And balance. That, too.

What an excellent day this would have been. The test and then freedom. Outcome outstanding. The Academy salutes. Oh, well done.

Saving the world was what Her thought we were doing. Well, maybe not the world, just us. Just our holes. Homes.

Horrors of the past repeated. Space shrinking, every year. We studied radioactivity in bones last year. And the glossary of extinct planetary phenomena.

Now Fire Lizard runs through The Checklist. What areas to be applied, what particular areas?

Her found me. Or I found Her. Huddled in hives, but we still knew the use of our hands and tongues. No one taught us. That fits here, and that fits there. You see? Like parts of a puzzle. Male and female. We need each other to complete. The feeling banishes all thought. You'll never make it out.

My father said he'd been a farmer once. He knew fruit trees, could describe them even though mother said he was making that up.

I knew to study. Look at what happens when they apply The Rule of Nobody. Space is limited, no room for Nobody. Study hard, boy, that's it. Forget Her.

Am I surprised Big would do that? To Her? No, I'm not surprised.

The Directive said: Your family will be fed and clothed. The Rule of Nobody will not apply.

I lean against a wall. I can still hear Fire Lizard: Here, we identify the 'Normal.' We identify the cutting edge of Average. Our past transgressions.

The inappropriateness of the action! I mean, the grabbing of the braid! For non-compliance!

Must be something we can do!

Yes, doubtless I need a bath.

The footsteps, back and forth in the classroom. The shoving of desks, the silence in the center where Her lies face down on her desk. The dragging sound as they lift Her.

Terror.

Her's shoes were purple. She loved the color.

Who started The Rule of Nobody? What was the first case? And the first cause? When? Which century? How many centuries ago?

Hives of activity. Mistrust leaks out, like rust.

Secrets. Don't ever let them find out, Her says.

Human nature, after all. To mess it all up. How we abhor the uniform.

Safety in numbers. They'll never find out. Something like that. The herd. The human organism has proven itself completely willful. The human organism is a complete narcissist. Narcissism results in confusion. My present condition.

And the consequences? The consequences of this confusion?

Well, extinction.

That niggling pain, right at the base of the skull.

Grab. Press.

Sparse terrain needs re-population. There used to be thousands here. How much longer?

I am ten, then I am twenty, then I am thirty. Then I have to
stop counting. A hundred years from now . . . but what is it all for?
Who remembers Her? Or us?

51

$$- 0 -$$

FIRST CAUSES

Class begins.

Fire Lizard tells us to turn on our cornea slips. "Today's topic," Fire Lizard says, "is First Causes."

We nod. The slips engage. Mine are still a bit fuzzy. Tears can do that to you.

Fire Lizard says, "Ku-Ling went so and so and did so and so and so and so happened. Clear?"

"Alpha to Omega, clear as clear," Big says.

I keep thinking about Her. What happened to Her yesterday. Oh, calamity. Oh, waste. (Discussion of the First Corollary: What is average is perfect. Thoughts dark as dark. Big arguing with Her. But, but, but. Her winking at me behind his back. Me thinking: Sunlight and glass. All muddiness now.)

If Her were in class, she would laugh and say something like *Kiloppety, Kiloppety you, oh Dragonheady.* Something to make me smile and ease my breath out.

Her used to tell me: *Somebody always wins. Somebody always loses.* Yesterday, Her lost. Everything.

We shared memories, Her and I. Now those are gone. Like Her. Poof!

Again, the waste. The pointlessness.

New student. In Her's seat. I can't look. She says to call her Knot.

Drinker says, "And what of the etc.?"

Fire Lizard curses softly: "Jee-zus. You thick."

"Glittering generality," I mumble.

Big says, turning to face me, "—*the fuck* you going on about now?"

"Unacceptable, what transpired here yesterday," I say.

Suddenly Fire Lizard yells, from the front of the room, "Explain. Corroborate. Do *not* postulate."

Behind me, Knot makes an ominous, hissing noise. I don't turn my head.

"Dragon's gone Foggy Brain," Drinker says with a smirk. "All over a girl. Over *Her*."

"Quiet!" Fire Lizard screams. His scrawny neck is stretched to the utmost. "Quiet, or bend!"

Big and Drinker giggle.

"They're loafing," I tell Fire Lizard.

"And you," Fire Lizard sputters, "are a japing fool."

Drinker guffaws.

"I agree," I say. "I am a japing fool."

"Shall I fiddle for you?" Fire Lizard resumes in his normal tone of voice. "Dance? Tra-la, Tra-la, Tra-la?"

"Dragon is milky-brained cause of Her," Big tells Fire Lizard. "He craves Her. Like poison."

"Fallacy," I say.

"Change is difficult," Fire Lizard says, for the first time looking at me with something like sympathy. "Disruptive. Care for a memory wipe? Or a yellow pill?"

"Show of hands," Big says. "To expel or not."

"We shall continue on the subject," Fire Lizard says. "Yes. Yes. Yes."

I know one thing, sure as sun will rise tomorrow: Her isn't coming back. That's my issue.

Fire Lizard asks: "Hydraulics and pulleys and suns. What happens?"

Knot clears her throat. "Trick question."

"Yes?" Fire Lizard says. "Is there more?"

"Drop all the way," Knot says.

"To where," Fire Lizard says. "And mind, next time, speak in complete sentences."

"Drop into the sea."

"Intelligence is a wonderful thing," Fire Lizard says, with a smirk. "Only one sea, is there? Next!"

They keep telling us, the expedition. You're here for the expedition. Three others and me. We each of us, mongrels. That's how I see it. That's how Her saw it.

Yesterday we four but Big vanished Her. So now there's Knot, and me, and Drinker, and Big. We four again. No need to say more. Past endurance.

A while later.

We're talking about walls. I think.

"How thick?" Fire Lizard asks.

"Three times twelve," Drinker says, and snickers.

"How thick?" Fire Lizard screams.

"A meter!" I scream back.

"And how high?" Fire Lizard's still screaming. Everyone in the room goes silent.

Finally, Knot speaks: "Thirty meters? At least?"

Fire Lizard's shoulders slump.

There's a bluish-greenish shadow on Big's back, right between his shoulder blades. I see it when he disrobes for inspection.

What is the cause, I think. Is it Tumor? Is it Plague? Is it Virus?

Big looks quickly behind and I turn my head away, but not quick enough.

"You!" Big says. "Foggy Brain. Come here!"

I tremble, rooted.

"Say," Big says. "Say 'I drink piss.'"

"Not I."

The connection is immediate. There's ringing in my ears for days.

In class we learn how all things green burnt up. Green grass burnt up. Trees burnt up.

We learn how mountains were cast into the sea. And why the sea became blood.

And why Creatures died.

And then the First Man, Ku-Ling, fell from Above. And he brought with him seeds (Where? In his pockets? No, can't be). Life. First Life.

New orders from the Head: Everyone has to work double shifts. More air, more oxygen, more effort.

I'm assigned to X, the south terminal. Big works there, too. Rather, Big pretends to work.

Early morning, we're just loading, he's already glaring at me.

"— you on about now?" he growls.

"Smell. I smell some'at. Don't you?"

"Oh?" A crafty look in Big's eyes.

"Burning. Something burning. Anomaly."

I'm peering, best I can. Hard when the lout is right there. Which he always is. Chewing his fingernails. *Don't be stupid, Dragon.* Her saying, in my head: *Patience, yeah?*

I lean my head against the wall. Tired.

"Quit skittering around," Big says. "Begone, else."

"Else?"

"Blood."

I nod. My cornea slip engages: "Engineer Dragon. Reporting Anomaly. X Level 5. Anomaly X Level 5."

Already I can see it: a spreading watery fire. Smoke begins to rise.

Big stands, fear swimming in his eyes. He shouts, "Oh, you fucker! You fucker!"

I'm shaking. Big's round, stupid face glowers. He nods and screams, "Over-ride! Repeat, over-ride! False report. There is no anomaly."

"Don't!" I cry. "Or we all crash."

"Now see here, Mumble-Face, we're already crashing. All of us."

I speak frantically: "Anomaly Level 5. Request assistance." After a beat, I add: "Urgent."

The only response I get is the crackle of static. White noise. It fills my ears, drowning me.

Big starts walking towards me. His voice drops. "Now, now, now, now. Is this payback? For what I did to Her? Her was a stray. Made me look like a clump. You another. Know what I do to strays? You stupid, fucking Fog Brain! I'll rip you in half!"

Wake up, Dragon! Wake up!

I swallow. It's Her!

Finish the game. So near the end now. Fucking lip-splitter's dying. He is. Finish him! No more fear. I'm here.

– 0 –

FLIGHT

My family lived in a three-story white house, built to resemble a ship, on the main street in Bacolod. That house rocked gently on its foundations. The windows were round, like portholes.

When I was still very young, I became obsessed with flying. I remember my first attempt. I was not even five. I thought I could sail through the air by simply spreading my arms. The first time I fell was from a balcony on the third story. Naturally, I fell hard. That was my first lesson: I ceased attempting to fly from such a great height. I made smaller, more successful attempts: from the front porch, and later, as I gained in confidence, from the second floor.

My mother had a great fear of my catching pneumonia. She had a younger sister, Candida, who developed a bad cold and then died in a hospital. She was just seven.

As the months passed, my wings itched terribly. I was assailed by temptation, almost every waking moment. For a long time, all I could manage were short distances, and only when I was sure I was not being observed. My mother began coming to my bed each night, cheeks wet with tears. The drops fell freely on my face. I lay under my blanket, wondering what I had done.

On my sixth birthday, wings began to sprout from between my shoulder blades. Hard, like sails.

My grandfather taught me. First, he said, one must have air. This is necessary to generate the required lift.

Then, the air must churn at a uniform rate. 100 cycles a minute was the minimum to raise my body two inches off the ground.

Third, my grandfather said, one must have optimism, for optimism infects the whole being, and renders it light.

Fourth, and this was absolutely essential: one must have light. My grandfather could only fly on clear, cloudless days. Light had an effect on his buoyancy.

When I was eight, my grandfather, by then a widower, developed a strange longing to live in Sweden. One morning, he put on his white *Americana* and boarded a small plane that would take him hopping through the continents. His pilot was his youngest son, my Uncle Dino. I never saw either my grandfather or my Uncle Dino, ever again.

In the beginning, my grandfather wrote every month. His letters from Sweden were cold: holding one was like holding a block of ice between my fingers. As soon as I finished reading a page, it would turn into snow. By the time I read the last page, a little pile of snow had collected at my feet. I would look up at the coconut palms that surrounded our house and feel my wings begin to unfurl. Then I would catch my mother looking at me through her bedroom window on the third floor. My wings trembled and remained shut tight.

Sometimes, I would talk to Father Naidro about my grandfather and his cold letters and my mother looking at me from her bedroom window and the snow collecting at my feet and my ambition to be the first Filipino to fly to Sweden, entirely unaided.

Father Naidro understood ambition: his older brother was the President. Father Naidro had entered the seminary to escape a similar fate. The brother immediately after him became a congressman.

Father Naidro was a priest, but he had never completely lost desire. At night, he told me, he dreamt he was a ship. Not a ship like the Don Julio, which carried passengers back and forth between the islands. No, he dreamt he was a Spanish galleon traveling across the Pacific to Mexico. Because he, in fact, was the ship, there was no crew, no one directing him where to go. In his dreams, he stopped at any number of islands. They had feminine names: Santa Catalina. Santa Imaculada, Santa Oa.

I objected to Santa Oa.

Father Naidro would say: All right, you name the island.

I thought for a while. Okay, I would say. Keep "Oa."

Father Naidro wanted to build a new church for Bacolod, because the old one had been damaged during a typhoon. The winds had knocked down the bell tower, which had been constructed of thick red brick, bricks that had withstood centuries of earthquakes and tropical humidity. The pile of bricks from the dilapidated tower made Father Naidro so sad that when he said Mass, his voice sank to a whisper, and all the parishioners had to murmur to keep up his spirits. Finally, my father gave a sizeable donation—almost 10 million pesos—for the repairs.

I could talk to Father Naidro whenever I liked.

One day, just before Christmas, my grandfather wrote:

I've moved down to the beach.

A year later, there was another letter:

I made it to Ystad. I am in good shape, I think. Shoulders ache. Thinking of exchanging wings for something more efficient.

I didn't understand. I counted back in my head and estimated that my grandfather was at least 60. He had been a widower for 15 years. Why hadn't he found another wife, there in Sweden? Surely there were any number of native women who would have been happy to spend two decades of their lives with someone who could fly?

Why did he want to exchange his wings for something else?

That was the last letter my grandfather ever wrote.

Several months later, around Easter, there was a letter from my Uncle Dino:

I live in a small village called Boras. Do you know it? If you take out a map of Sweden, it is lower down, near the point where two great rivers meet. My wife's name is Karin. She knows no other language but Swedish.

The very last sentence of my Uncle's letter was:

Father passed away two days ago at 8:30 in the morning.

I wanted to know why. I wanted to know what had happened. Why did my uncle reserve the news about my grandfather till the very end? Was he sorry? How would he cope with his terrible loneliness?

It so happened that when my grandfather's will was unsealed, in the law offices of my father's old schoolmate, Señor Isagani, I was found to be the sole inheritor of all my grandfather's land. I had become a landowner, with possession of all our family's farms, which stretched from one end of our island to the other.

I decided that the best way to oversee my new possessions was to fly. This time I made no secret of my skill. I flew just above the trees that marked the boundaries of each farm. The people who worked for us at tilling the soil stopped and stared. A few, however, recognized me and waved.

My father grew preoccupied. The liquid in his dinner glass was always a light amber color, which deepened with the passing years.

One night, he passed me a note. His fingers, I remember, were dry as paper. The note said:

Go, sell what thou hast, and give it to the poor, and thou shalt have treasure in Heaven.

I looked at my father, but in his face there was no sign, no reassurance.

I flew over greater and greater distances. I saw the rocky shores of the southernmost islands. I heard the sea people lamenting the passing of time on their gray rocks. I heard the angels singing, just above the clouds.

It was now very painful to walk. My feet developed blisters more readily. I took care to remain just a few inches above the ground.

When I had grown fully into my manhood, the wings began to pain me. Especially at night, when I lay on my bed. I tossed and turned. I imagined my father listening in the dark. I suspected his satisfaction when, the next morning, at the breakfast table, I appeared with shadows under my eyes.

My grandfather had left some personal effects in the safekeeping of Father Naidro. Father Naidro kept my grandfather's papers and his collection of pipes in a carved ivory chest underneath his bed. He did not want to show me the contents of the ivory chest, not at first. Eventually, when I persuaded him to trust me, he laid in my arms a great quantity of photographs, all of my grandfather as a young man, before he had married. His wings were enormous, even larger than mine.

I decided that I would, in time, write a book about my grandfather. One day, when I was 40, I did write a book.

After my mother read it, she said: Your grandfather was a myth.

Yes, I replied. But he is a myth that turns out to be true.

So, what is a true myth, my mother asked. She added: It reminds me of the stories of *aswang* my nursemaid used to tell me, when she wanted me to behave. How they come out of the dark, with the forked tongues. And suck the blood of infants.

He is a story, I said to my mother. Not a myth. And I will continue writing until I can't begin anymore.

– 0 –

THE HAND

She had been married quite a long time, almost 18 years, to a man who, in the last year or two, had begun to spend most of his time watching TV. When they were first married, when they were both in graduate school, they had started out with a small black-and-white.

Eventually, after perhaps the 6th year of their marriage, her husband had agreed to buy a small colored TV. Finally, just two years ago, they had gotten another TV so that she could watch her favorite shows without having to wait for her husband to finish watching a football game.

In the last couple of years, time seemed to be moving very fast, seemed almost to be accelerating, and the more she tried to hold on to it, the less of it there was to hold. This was a frightening feeling, a feeling she tried over and over to analyze. On this particular Monday evening, a light rain was falling. She could hear the gentle sound of the drops against the trees outside her window.

This morning the rain made her happy, since it reminded her of her childhood in the Philippines, when the yellowish glow from the low-watt bulbs made the rooms look unearthly, and everything in them blurred, as though she were looking at her surroundings from underwater. She remembered sitting at the round table in the kitchen, which was her favorite room in the house, where she sat surrounded by the bustling maids, the sound of people entering and leaving.

All day the question had been inside her, waiting.

Her husband was sitting on the couch. She could just make out part of his nose in profile. He'd come home only an hour earlier, his hair slick with the rain. He had his face turned toward the TV, which this evening was showing an episode of *9-1-1*.

When was it that she had noticed the hand? The hand that was just a hand, nothing else, reaching out to tap him on his shoulder.

Now she recalled seeing it for the first time the Friday before. She'd given herself a shake, rubbed her eyes, looked again. Yes, there was most unmistakably a hand, reaching out just above her husband's right shoulder. The index finger was extended, pointing downwards. She anticipated the moment of physical contact and held her breath. But the hand—a woman's hand, she realized suddenly— remained suspended, frozen, as it were, just above and behind her husband.

She tried to circle around it, to observe it more closely. When she got within a foot, she stopped, fearing she would alarm her husband, who was absorbed, as usual, in some TV show that involved many people running around and shouting.

The hand had a faint tracery of blue veins spreading, fan-like, from a narrow wrist. It was preternaturally white, a white like the bellies of the dead fish piled up in front of the stalls at the wet market back home in Manila. The pearl-colored nails were oval in shape. She mused about who the hand's owner might be: perhaps a young woman, someone 10 or even 15 years younger than herself. What was it being communicated to her husband? Why was she here? Teresa didn't know. The need to know, however, was like an ache. So palpable, she could almost feel it behind her teeth when she went to bed that night.

Later that afternoon, she had the accident. She was making a slow right turn onto El Camino Real when she felt the thud on her rear bumper. Everything in the car went flying: CDs, books, her handbag. Her head hit something—hard. She lay on her side for what seemed like long moments, looking upwards at her feet. A trickle of something wet ran down the right side of her face. From far, far away, she heard indistinct voices. "An accident," she thought.

"Something has happened."

She tried to say something. "Please help me." And, a little later, "Am I dying?" But there was no one to speak to. Her gaze was entirely directed now on a square of cracked window through which she saw—smelled—hot asphalt and, occasionally, a glimpse of running feet in heavy-soled boots.

"Wait," she told herself. "Just wait."

She could taste blood in her mouth—salty, not unlike tears. Her face was wet. A hand appeared at the window. Lined and creased, with dirt along the grooves of the palm. It gestured, implored.

"I can't," she said. "Can't." Can't move, was what she wanted to say.

If only she had been able to speak.

The hand continued its pleas. It was moving faster now, up and down, as if trying to communicate a matter of great urgency. "I—" she said. "I—" She could see her own hand, palm upraised, lying on the street. But she felt nothing, not the asphalt underneath it, which looked rough and hot, or the thing someone—a passerby?—had placed into her limp fingers, which she recognized as a simple wooden rosary.

Finally, she managed to say, with great effort, "My husband."

"What?" A disembodied voice. A male voice.

She couldn't think anymore. She let her head drop and closed her eyes.

She felt movement now, around her. Someone was lifting. Or she was being lifted. A great groaning. How awful that sound was. Metal grinding against metal.

There was a rush of air. She opened her eyes. She saw sky. Blue. Gray. She was free! She tried to wiggle her fingers. She felt nothing. A strange lassitude came over her after the effort.

She was not going to die here, right now, on this street. She wanted to taste—ice cream. Something. Cold. Sweet. Her tongue probed ineffectually at the roof of her mouth. Impossibly dry. Again she tried to work her fingers.

She found herself looking down at her skirt, which was stained with great swathes of purple dye. Purple dye? Hadn't this been a beige skirt when she'd put it on this morning? What did this mean? What did this all mean?

Was she dying?

Or was she, in fact, living, and was that what the purple dye all over her beige skirt was trying to tell her? That life was living. Was going on. Even though the white hand on her husband's shoulder this morning had seemed to say: Die. Die. I want you to die. Fate, luck, chance had put her in the way of the car that had so conveniently hit her bumper. Hit her hard enough to kill her. But, unlucky as always, she had survived. She was now alive. This was the unintended consequence. This was life.

And so what to do now? She thought this even as they were putting her on the gurney (which bumped terribly over the uneven asphalt of the street, she nearly cried out but stopped herself just in time, just as the scream was about to escape from between her teeth), even as she saw the straps come down on either of her arms, saw a swaying bottle of fluid on a flexible pole affixed next to her arm.

She wondered what it all meant: the hand over her husband's shoulder, the gray clouds spitting rain, the accident . . .

She recalled her husband's last words to her, spoken only this morning, before he'd left for work: Tell your son we're not going to get him a new car. Their only child was at college in Los Angeles. The weekend before, while driving up for her birthday, he'd had an accident. His car, an old Civic with nearly 200,000 miles, was irreparable. Or so the nearest mechanic, the only one he could tow the wreck to, had said. The car was so old, so decrepit, that she'd secretly been glad at the news. Perhaps now her husband would consent to help their son get a better car. One with a more durable body that would not crumple at the first impact with another vehicle.

But all her husband said at the news was no, no, let him take the train up. We can't afford to get him another car.

Teresa had not anticipated the hurt that arose in her at these words. She herself would have given anything—her right arm—to help her son have what she knew he desired most of all. But she had been unable to summon the right words. She had kept silent, and eventually her husband had left, toting his heavy briefcase and walking toward his car the way she imagined someone might who was only marking time.

And now this scene was playing over and over in her head, as the ambulance raced through traffic.

"What did you say?" said a young man in white who happened to be sitting next to her.

She stared at him. Shook her head.

He came closer.

No, no! She wanted to yell. Keep away! The smell of him was almost overwhelming—a smell of sweet aftershave and sweat. It brought her back, almost all the way back. To the present moment—what was she doing lying flat on her back in this crazily swaying vehicle—where she had no intention of staying, not if she could help it.

"You will—" she said, after a while.

"What?" he said again.

Was he completely stupid?

She shook her head.

"Can you speak up a little, ma'am? What do you want?" he said.

This time she was angry. The anger was pulling her mouth down at the corners, she could feel it. She could also imagine her face, as she stared at this young man, the lines deepening on either side of her jaw. What a sight she must be. What a fright she must look.

What—

Now the man reached over and brushed something cool and wet over her face. Ahhh, she thought. *Do it again.*

But he'd sat back. Now he was simply staring at her.

"My fingers?" she asked him.

He looked at her hands.

"They're fine," he said.

"Rub," she requested.

She could see him put his hands below. But she felt nothing. Tears came spilling out of her eyes. Her mouth opened helplessly.

"You will be fine, all right? Ma'am?" he said. He was impatient with her. Because she was old. She knew this in her heart. The old were like residents of another country. Here they were treated like children, to whom everything must be explained.

What she wanted, what she had always wanted, if she'd had the sense to know this, when she was alive, before, was to go to that place she knew existed, if only in herself. It was so long ago, but she'd been there. She'd inhabited this magical realm with all of her being. During a time before her son was born, before her marriage, even. Sunlight moved there. And talahib. Wild grass. Outside her bedroom window, while she watched, in the late afternoon—birds, snakes, little boys.

The house that was to have been built there had never been built. So a pile of rubble had been left in the vacant lot—a small hill of rubble. Then, the rains had come, and the grass had come, and after that the birds, and still after that the snakes, and last of all were the little boys with their slingshots and their makeshift pellet guns and then the bringing of small animals to her, the daughter of the big house next door.

Once, they brought a downy chick. "Where is the mother?" she asked her yaya to ask them. The yaya asked. The boys only covered their mouths with their hands and giggled.

And when she was in high school and had to do science projects, when she needed specimens to dissect in the lab, they gladly brought her dead snakes which she poured into glass bottles, covering their inert forms with formaldehyde. Once the little boys brought her the carcass of a puppy and she almost screamed. White and still, its long silky white hair matted with mud. That, too, she eventually put in a bottle and stuck in the freezer, behind the milkfish and the frozen cow innards.

The boys—their soft, whispery voices, their large dark eyes—had looked at her with awe. All because she wore the uniform of the convent school and spoke in perfect English. Because she had a *yaya* and lived in a two-story house with a tiled roof.

The *yaya*, a girl of 16, had come straight from the provinces. She never questioned what Teresa asked her to do. She was supremely patient, and kind, and Teresa had never understood why in the end her mother had fired her. Teresa had seen the yaya sobbing as she packed her meager things into a plastic case, so perhaps the girl had committed some great shame.

That was a long time ago. In fact, until this very moment, she'd forgotten all about the yaya and the boys who brought her animals. She'd grown old, and had left that sleepy island, that small city—was this why she had grown old? Yes, perhaps—and it had been a long time since anyone had looked at her that way. Maybe not since she had taken up residence in California. But now she suddenly remembered the *yaya's* name: It was Juliet. A smile broke out on her lips. Yes, her name was Juliet.

Why was she thinking of this now, while lying in the madly swaying ambulance, while looking at the profile of the young man who was looking, seemingly bored, out the window? She was a carcass on a gurney. She had known this feeling many times before, and now it had truly happened.

They released her from the hospital after a week. They wheeled her to her husband in a wheelchair. He looked down at her with something like impatience. Slowly, gingerly, she lifted herself into the car. The air was hot; dust speckled her eyelids. She felt as if little needles were stinging her eyes. She clutched at her husband's arm but after a while she released her fingers.

He drove her home. She looked out the window, at the bare trees of a cold day. It's November already, she thought. Neither of them spoke.

"Can you make it up the stairs by yourself? I'm late for work," her husband said. She nodded, yes. He helped her up to the front step but then turned to go. Slowly, very slowly, she ascended the stairs. Now and then she stopped to rest. She became short of breath. Her weakness frightened her. She stopped halfway up.

In bed at night, sometimes, after her husband was asleep, she would get up on one elbow and look at him. Her husband's eyes were closed, his breathing even, but now and then he would shudder, and this shudder was so deep, so seemingly from somewhere mysterious and hidden, that it made her afraid.

In the morning, he would give no indication that he was aware that anything had passed between them in the night.

Since the hand had appeared, it usually lay on her husband's chest when he was sleeping. She hated the sight of it, like a white dead thing, in the moonlight from the window. Where was her husband now? He was far away, in a glass building next to many other glass buildings, so many close together that it was impossible for her to tell them apart. In these buildings, engineers worked, and technicians, and other people associated with industry, and they were all very busy preparing reports.

Even if it was a beautiful day, and there were many, in this part of the country, no one, she was sure, would be able to leave for more than an hour, to have lunch. She thought that it was a great waste, a great pity. She would hate to die after having lived for years in such a life.

And now the thought came to her that her husband would not even know whom to call, on her behalf, if some further mishap befell her. Unless she told him. There was her son, of course, and her mother in the Philippines, but who else? And what if she were hurt in such a way that she could not speak, could not get the words out? Her husband would have to look in her wallet, or her checkbook, and even these would tell him nothing.

If she needed to be brought again to the hospital, someone might notice her ring and say, "She has a husband." How would they find him? Would he eventually come, looking disheveled and confused, and be angry with her? She could imagine him sitting across from her and asking, "What have you done now?" in that familiar, exasperated tone of voice. Even though he could see her lying with tubes affixed to both arms and perhaps her throat. The hand might still be with him, and she knew by now that no one else could see it, only herself.

Hours later, it really did happen the way she had imagined, with only slight differences. That is, her husband did come home, looking fairly disheveled, and he did sit across from her on the bed, and that very same question she had imagined he would ask did come out of his mouth: "What have you done now?" And yes, there it was, hovering behind his shoulder, the hand, the hand which now bore a faint trace of scent, not "White Diamonds" exactly, more like "Charlie" or "Je Reviens," something girlie and cheap.

Her husband's face was guarded, he was wearing a green sweater spotted with rain. His hair was wet.

He was talking about the accident now, asking how did this happen, how did you manage to get yourself into such a situation?

Really, it was too funny. She had slipped, she had knocked her head on something sharp, there was a swelling above her right eye. This was the face she presented to her husband when he arrived home, later that night. She had to keep looking over her husband's shoulder, she couldn't help it. She wanted the hand to go away but it was resting on her husband's shoulder and playing with the hair at the back of his head.

Can't he feel it pulling? Doesn't it tickle his ear?

She couldn't answer him, of course—there was a tube in her mouth hooked up to a large machine. The tube was stretching her lips apart and flattening them and she imagined she must look ugly. The doctor had held a whispered conversation with her husband— right in front of her! But in a voice so low she couldn't make out the sense of the words. Now something leaked out of the corners of her eyes, but her husband didn't seem to notice.

He was rubbing his forehead and saying, "I will have to call the insurance agent. The car—completely totaled . . ."

And yes, she knew this was a terrible thing. The money, the insurance, the higher premiums . . . She couldn't help it, she was so easily distracted. It might have been a movement out of the corner of her eye, some gust of wind shaking the trees by the side of the road. Or a girl's red sweater, flashing brightly as she sailed by on a ten-speed. Something that looked like happiness. Yes, she was so easily distracted.

When she looked up again, the chair where her husband had sat, seemingly just moments before, was empty. The room had a strange light; eventually she recognized it as sunlight streaming weakly in through the drawn curtains. She thought: I must have fallen asleep. A whole night must have passed, therefore, in this strange state. Now it was morning. Her husband had probably gone home. An image flashed through her mind: her husband getting into his white car, impervious to the light rain speckling his graying hair. And now it would be close to the time for his alarm clock to go off. He would be getting up soon, getting his things together to go to the office.

It seemed amazing to her that she had managed to fall asleep, in that state, in that place. Where she knew no one. She recognized in herself a terrible thirst. But there was nothing within reach—no glass, no water. Mingled with the great thirst was a feeling of abandonment. She knew this feeling; it had been common enough throughout her marriage. The sight of the empty chair bothered her. She turned her head to avoid looking at it.

And then she saw the little thing. How could she have forgotten—? It was close to her now, snuggled on the sheets by her right hip. It lay quite still.

She looked at it again. So still it could have been a spider, resting there. There was nothing she could do.

She groaned. The sound, so deep, startled her. A machine with blinking red lights began to beep softly. She stifled any further noise.

She determined to get up, right that instant, to undo the tracery of tubes that fed her veins with a colorless liquid, to escape the softly beeping monitor. "All right," she whispered. Manfully she threw her legs over the side of the bed. She positioned her hands, palms downward, on either side of her. As if preparing for a final effort. A young nurse was standing at the foot of the bed, staring at her. The nurse's expression was cold, even hostile. She said nothing, however. The nurse might have been made of cardboard, so stiffly did she stand there, a clipboard cradled in her right arm.

The hand beckoned her forward.

– 0 –

SOFIA

Sofia had broad shoulders and large feet which reminded everyone who knew her of her deceased father. Her face had a perpetually anxious, questioning look. She spoke little and was often seen to be reading—either a newspaper or a magazine or a book she had checked out from the library. She was considered a woman of pure and unblemished spirit, one whose name had never been sullied by unsavory gossip—no never, not even when she was much younger and had been considered pretty.

She lived in a dusty town on a Philippine island. Next to her house was the cemetery where Sofia's parents, grandparents, and siblings had been laid to rest. Wonderful Sofia! Whose intuition and perspicacity had been honed to such a fine point during her long life, during a life that had been spent, mostly, in avoiding excitement, and hence, shame. All these decades, no one had whispered things about her.

As far as admirers, she had had two. She had no idea what qualities had attracted these boys. They were shy, the kind who read books and wrote poetry and felt better if they treated a woman with gentleness. Since nothing about them excited her, after a few dull outings, which vexed Sofia because she realized she had nothing she wished to share, the boys shrank back. The boys saw, despite Sofia's careful words, despite her reticence, the look in her eyes that said, *You will be making a mistake.*

Then, when she turned 50, Sofia realized that she could do whatever she liked, have a man or men over, have them stay late, and no one would suspect her of indiscretion. Because she had become old. She was beyond thought.

The story begins when Sofia is just a week shy of her 54th birthday. It was the first morning in many weeks that it had not rained. Sofia was impatient to start pruning her roses: she always completed this chore by Valentine's Day. She enjoyed caressing the twiggy canes, feeling for the fat, swollen buds, the ones she had coaxed full of reddish nodes, full almost to bursting.

The man who visited her that day was wearing a white suit. He came up quietly and stood there for a few moments, watching. It took Sofia a few moments to sense his presence: he was so quiet, as if he had glided rather than walked. He was actually standing very close to her, less than a foot away.

He was not a good-looking man. Neither was he an ugly man. Sofia had a feeling that he was not old—though his thick hair was a stunning white—but neither was he young. He possessed an air of gravity, but there was a kind of restlessness in his eyes.

When she was almost 40, not yet old, she had chosen a man. There was no one but herself to blame. For once in her life, Sofia had thought, for once in her life, let her experience without fear.

Yes, she had experienced. It was very brief: only a few weeks. The man was overwhelmed with guilt, with thoughts about his pretty wife, waiting for him at home. It was the most base sort of sneaking around. They had even, once, rented a motel room for a few hours in the middle of the day. The man had lied to his boss and said he needed to visit his ailing mother in some far-away province.

After the second week of their affair, he acted as though he were disgusted with Sofia. He stopped calling. Sofia tried waiting for him outside his home. She caught a glimpse of him in his living room: he and his wife were sitting together on the couch, which faced the picture window. The wife's head was resting on the man's shoulder. Sofia observed the expression of contentment on the wife's face and in her half-closed, almost-dreaming eyes. Sofia saw that her lover was happy in his home, and that when he embraced his wife he was gentle. As Sofia hurried home, she realized what a fool she'd been. She did not try to contact the man again.

Several years after this, there was a young girl who Sofia had allowed to be a kind of companion. The girl had a family that, she said, mistreated her. Her mother was jealous and made her daughter have meals in the kitchen with the maids. Her name was Lucy.

Lucy was always running to Sofia, overwhelmed with fear and anxiety. Sofia wondered to herself, What is it, what is it about this girl? The girl, in spite of the great difference in their ages, seemed to enjoy conversing with Sofia. She loved looking at Sofia's wonderful books, most of which were biographies of free-spirited women, like Cleopatra, Isadora Duncan, and Frida Kahlo. It had felt natural for Sofia to invite her to stay in one of the rooms of the large, empty house. The girl brought her things over, just two days later. Then she began hanging up her own paintings, hammering late into the night. When the girl went out, Sofia sometimes peeked into the room, to assess the damage to the walls.

The paintings were posters of Impressionists like Degas and Monet. They were clumsily framed and when Sofia tilted them so that she could inspect the walls behind, she found that Lucy had changed her mind more than once: a constellation of small holes lay behind each frame. Sofia was annoyed but said nothing.

There were further discoveries. Lucy liked to wander around the house in her underwear. It startled Sofia to realize that the girl had a sensuous figure. When a man came to fix the leaky kitchen faucet, Lucy was standing at the stove, in a short, white dress that gave ample view of her white, heavy thighs. When the man appeared in the kitchen, Lucy showed not the least embarrassment. Sofia thought: what have I gotten myself into? The man stared at the girl openly, with admiration. Sofia caught that look directed at the girl.

After a brief nod to acknowledge the man's presence, Lucy
had turned her back to them and nonchalantly resumed stirring
something on the stove. Sofia could not see Lucy's face but she saw,
in the slight adjustment Lucy had made in her stance, in Lucy's
pronouncedly languid movements, that the girl felt pride.

Oh! It was Sofia who was embarrassed, though whether for
herself or for Lucy, she could not say. Sofia stepped away, telling
the man that she would be in the living room if he needed her. She
sat on her flowered couch, her back very straight, and tried not to
listen to the silence that seeped out of the kitchen, where Lucy
stood at the stove and the man crouched under the sink.

She felt—no, knew—that she was invisible to them.

The following week, Lucy and Sofia had an argument. Lucy
had allowed a male visitor to spend the night. Not the man who
fixed the kitchen faucet—another, much older, man. Sofia guessed
the man was married. Lucy said No.

The next day, when Sofia happened to wander into the girl's
room, the paintings were gone and the bare walls, with their
clusters of holes, were horrifying. Sofia had sat on the bed, whose
sheets were rumpled and still smelled of Lucy, of her sweat and her
secrets. She got up eventually and closed the door to the room. She
did not enter it again for almost a year, and then all she did was
strip the bed of its soiled sheets, and open a window, wide.

Sofia pretended at first not to notice the stranger. Eventually,
however, without pausing in her pruning, with her head carefully
turned away from him, she said, "I did not call you. Why are you
here?"

"I never wait to be called," the man said. "You must know
that."

Yes, she knew. But she was weak. And just a little afraid.

She said, "To have had a child—that would have been nice."

The white-haired stranger nodded gravely, as if he were in complete agreement.

Sofia did not believe in A Great Being. She had read Dostoevsky, Flaubert, Hugo, Tolstoy, Dickens, Thomas Hardy—she had nothing if not time on her hands. She had even read David Foster Wallace. These writers had convinced her to stop attending mass, to stop offering prayers.

When I die, she sometimes thought. *When I die—what? Nothing. There will be nothing.*

"I had expected a woman," Sofia said.

"I can be a woman, if you like," the man said. "If that would make this easier."

"Nothing can make this easier," Sofia said. She put down her pruning shears. The gesture made her sad. She said, turning to face the man, "You must be busy."

"This week has been very busy," the man said. "Mostly because of the typhoon."

Ah! Sofia remembered. On the island of Leyte, a whole city had been demolished, and with it thousands and thousands of people. Many had died under the rubble of the cathedral. Sofia dragged her mind back from the images of destruction. It was difficult.

"Where is my mother?" she asked suddenly. She had not thought of her mother in many years. This question surprised even herself.

"How is she?" Sofia asked. In truth, they had never been close. Sofia's three brothers had loved their mother with a fierce love that was returned, note for note. Sofia's love was a limp, passive thing. Her mother had brushed it off, as one would brush off a fly. When Sofia tried to recall her mother now, it shocked her to realize that she could remember only her mother's back, her long and sinewy back, and her mother's bony neck, and the hard knobs of her mother's shoulders, and the long, grey hair piled high on the very top of her head in a sloppy bun.

The man remained silent. Could he read Sofia's thoughts? Abruptly, he sat down on the green bench under the orange tree and began to loosen his tie. Sofia expected him to begin removing his coat, but he did not. The sun had made his face red.

"Why now?" she asked. She had not meant for her voice to tremble. *Have I been happy*, she wondered, then said aloud, "I wanted—but I was weak."

The man shrugged. "There is far too much emphasis on happiness," he said, "in this day and age."

"Did you have to travel far?" Sofia asked.

"No," the man said.

"The weariness," Sofia said, "made me think you had come a long way."

"Do not mistake my sympathy for weariness. For me, it is no trouble. Merely the motion of blinking an eye."

"I see," Sofia said. "And when I come with you now, will it also be as easy as that, like blinking an eye?"

"It will be a bit more troublesome, there may be a little pain. I have found that it always helps to relax the shoulders. But it will be quicker than you think."

"And what of my body? How shall it be arranged?" Sofia asked.

"Do not trouble yourself about that," the man said. "If you like, I will leave it here, under the orange tree."

"And my arms, how shall they be positioned? Crossed over my chest, as if I were praying? But I never pray. Should I fling out my arms, as if I were taken by surprise?"

"Flung out," the man said. "That always makes quite an impression."

"I wasn't aware I could be quite so dramatic," Sofia said.

The man's lips moved, but no sound issued forth.

"And my mouth—open or closed?"

"Open," the man said. "But just a little."

"I see," Sofia said. She thought for a few moments. "And what was the cause?"

"There is a small pistol in the shed, I believe," the man said.

Yes! Yes, she knew it. She had always known it.

"But I don't want people to see my teeth," Sofia said.

"What people think of your teeth is of no importance," the man said. "Indeed, it is of no importance even *now*."

"Right now, at this moment, I have moved on? Already?"

"In essence, yes. You are merely taking leave of your body. It does sometimes take time. People become attached to things that are really of no importance, that are merely unnecessary complications."

"I can still feel my arms and legs, the heat on my skin."

"Vestigial impulses. Nothing more. You are, in fact, seated right next to me, here, on the bench."

"Ah, not so much pain," Sofia said.

"You are quicker than most."

Sofia sat down. She glanced at her fingers. She was gripping a rose stem so tightly that she could see tiny points of blood beginning to emerge on the palms of her hands. But, no sooner had she taken note of them than the blood began, as if by magic, to vanish.

"It does not hurt," she said, wonderingly.

"You have your mother's hands," the man said.

"Who are you?" Sofia asked. "Are you a relative?"

"I am your great-great-great grandfather, once removed. My name is Basiliso."

"You were Spanish."

"Yes, but I was born right here, in the Islands."

"And what did you do?"

"I was a *platero*. You know? A silversmith."

Sofia gave a start.

"The friars collected the town's silver, and I fashioned them into lovely *karwahes* which were used to transport the figure of the Santo Niño during the Holy Week procession. People asked me how I was able to accumulate so much wealth, but I do not give away my secrets. Even now. Are you ready?"

"Not yet," Sofia said.

The man sighed. "You are stubborn."

"I wish someone had told me," she said.

"My dear, you ask far too much."

"I don't like to be taken by surprise."

"And that was always your trouble."

Sofia felt anger flash. "And how would you know what trouble is? You have never had a mother like mine."

"Ah, but I have. All women in our family are alike."

"My father was sad, when she passed."

"The women in our family are very charismatic. No one can resist them."

Sofia thought about that for a moment.

"It's been 20 years," she said. "He still keeps that picture of her, the one taken in Hong Kong, when they were on their honeymoon. He keeps it under his pillow in the Home."

"Why do you check? It is clear that your father loved your mother."

"He's had it there, ever since she died."

"You are fortunate, to have such a father."

"He doesn't remember anyone else."

Basiliso was silent.

"All right," Sofia said. "I am ready. Shall I lie down?"

"But you are down already. See?" Basiliso indicated a spot behind her. Sofia did not turn her head.

"I wish—," she said. The words hung. Sofia could no longer complete them.

"You wish you had more time."

"No. Not that."

Basiliso waited.

"Today, I read a book. It wasn't a very good book. I shouldn't have wasted my time with it. And, just a few minutes ago, I finished all the grapes in the white bowl on the kitchen counter. I was greedy, that was always my problem."

"Well—" the man cleared his throat. He did not continue.

"But I don't really like grapes. So why did I eat all of them?" When the man did not respond, Sofia said, wonderingly, "Food is life. That's why I ate them. Or perhaps I was feeling lonely. I always eat more when I'm lonely."

She went on. She couldn't stop talking. Perhaps it was the man's stillness. "I always hated my name. I wished I could have been named Serena, or Lily."

"Sofia is a beautiful name," the man said. "You are the only Sofia in our family. And you will be the only Sofia for two generations. You will be unique, for a while."

"Oh, it is good to know that there will be another," Sofia burst out. "Do names have any meaning—there?"

"No."

"What meaning, then? What meaning, if there are no names?"

"There is no sorrow."

"My life was not that unpleasant. The only complaint I have is the loneliness. Am I going to purgatory?"

"Purgatory! A figment of a friar's over-active imagination. There is no such thing."

"If I told a lie, in school, the nuns said I would end up in purgatory."

Basiliso snorted. It was an odd sound. But now Sofia saw that he no longer had a face, only a dull orb, where she had expected to see eyes, nose, mouth—something at least comfortingly familiar.

"I can't talk to you anymore; you have disappeared."

Basiliso answered; to Sofia it sounded like the dull roaring of the wind through the trees, in the aftermath of a storm.

She would not be happy in that other place, she knew. But not to have sorrow was a good thing. One cannot have everything. She stood. She wondered what she would say to her mother. She wondered: Who will find me?

Basiliso raised his right hand and lovingly touched Sofia's cheek. "My dear—" he said. "Why are you crying? There is absolutely nothing to be afraid of." The hand on her cheek felt gossamer thin, like a spray of fine mist from the ocean.

– 0 –

DOWN

"We're going down. We're going under."

"When?" I ask.

"Today."

"We don't have maps."

"We don't need maps. There's only one way to go, and that's down."

My right eye starts twitching. It moves up, down, to the side, as if driven by an invisible engine. Synaptic misfire! Oh, here comes the other one!

Of course, he says next, "Look at your funny little eyes."

Last night I had that dream again. Spiders and snakes. All around, spiders and snakes. There was a snake twice my height. I caught hold of it by the snout, stretched its mouth wide, wide. A very long, red tongue poked out. Then I woke up.

Things are the way they are today. I ask and ask and ask. They might not be here tomorrow. No, they'll definitely be gone tomorrow. Or we'll be.

We found one of those strange flopping things on the beach. It's always a bad day when we come across one of those.

I never look too closely. They're not fish. If we stay Surface, will there come a day we see something we recognize? The eyes of Weary Edward, or Anxious Alice.

We're all mostly water. If we relax, we'll float. We can't drown. A baby, you know, floats! I know!

I remember scratchy old film, people wearing Aqua-Lungs. They got in their silver wet suits and went exploring. I loved those.

"What's down there," he says, are people. The ones who've gone before."

"Right."

Don't you think the first ones to reach Bottom would want to share that with us Surface? What's down there is just wreckage, but I can't tell him that.

They used to show us maps. The Mariana Trench, they said. That's where we should go. Far from the abandoned nuclear plants. As far as we can get.

Now I remember: Viscor Vespucci. The self-described Explorer-at-Large. His fascination with dolphins and whales. Spent millions on subs that could get people deeper, ever deeper. Two years ago, he went Down. Not even one transmission after. Vanished. Years we spent waiting.

To physically enter that world . . .

He keeps telling me that if we stay here, we'll die. Or turn into one of those spider things, like Becky. I don't like to think of her that way, but then why was that creature wearing her sweater? He says, "The ocean is a gift."

I look at the sea. Pinki Pi bobs reassuringly by the marker buoy. I almost expect her to start singing. Pinki Pi, he'll say, give us climate stats for the Southern Hemisphere. Or: Pinki Pi, play the Beatles.

He's programmed her so that she can conceptualize the future: "If this happens, do this." He's taped his voice, at varying degrees of emotional pitch, and taught her how to tell the difference between his "distress" voice and his other ones.

I stare at Pinki Pi, swallow hard, and look away. I remember others like her. What happened to them? It's hard to get a fix on time when there's no one else following after you.

I tick off the distances: 60 meters? 150 meters? 200? Could even be 500.

I remember those old Mating Education films they used to show us. *How to copulate under water.* A naked man swims into the center of a group of naked women. The man is ready, he's unsheathed, he's ready to party! He starts grabbing women, left and right. My goodness!

"Evolutionary biology," the narrator intones. He looks over at me and starts winking.

He is stubborn. I'd rather stay Surface, if you don't mind. This little spot of beach is home now. Home, home, home.

I look up at the strange-colored sky. The air scorches.

How did we first meet? He had a wife, if I remember rightly. Something happened to her, something vaguely Alien popped out of her. Inter-species something. I'm always mixing things up with old movies. The mid-eighties, I think.

I am no butt-kicking Ripley.

Petrified. Thinking about Viscor Vespucci again. Always thinking about Viscor Vespucci. *"There are cities in the bottom of the ocean,"* Viscor told us. *"With people who look just like us."*

An assistant tapped him on the shoulder, in the middle of his speech! "Oh, is it time?" Viscor said. His face went very pale.

He had this old, old weapon, this old sub-machine gun, he carried it around everywhere. When he was about to go Down, he slung it over his shoulder and said, "All right. We're going to be O.K."

He'd spent years preparing.

I still picture the scene in my mind: Viscor moving towards his bathosphere, walking jerkily, the rest of us watching and mildly cheering.

When he got to the shore, Viscor turned one last time and said, "I'm living in the future now."

Cheers.

"If you want to know what happens in the future," I tell him, "just ask Viscor."

$$- 0 -$$

THE ESSENCE OF SPAIN

A year ago, I became convinced that I should spend the rest of my life in Spain.

I made up my mind to find the true, true essence of Spain.

I decided that, until I got to Spain, I would listen only to Camaron.

I purchased maps, because I had decided that one of the important things I had to do was walk the pilgrim road to Santiago de Compostela.

To prepare myself for the Spanish time clock, I disciplined myself not to eat until 10 p.m.

To get used to the idea of "siesta," I imposed a daily two-hour nap on my hectic life, which resulted in my employment being terminated, which made me happy because I had become extremely worried about exceeding vacation limits. Now, I could just go to Spain and stay as long as I wanted.

I imagined myself in a square surrounded on all sides by buildings with iron bars over the windows. At the very center of this square would be a fountain, and at the center of this fountain would be the statue of some eminently great person: Blas Infante or Julius Caesar.

I decided I would use only "usted" when addressing others, even if the other was someone obviously younger than myself.

I learned that in Spain they care greatly about appearances. I read this in the Travel section of The New York Times, which I bought at least once a week, to keep myself informed not only about Spanish customs, but about life in Europe in general.

I imagined myself threading through *calle* after *calle* after *calle*.

Once, on the subway, I sat across from a man who was reading *El Pais*. I stared at him so long that eventually he looked up. When he saw who it was staring, he lifted his newspaper so that it almost covered his entire face.

I will learn to make the sign of the crucifix every time I pass a cemetery or a church.

I will be wary of Gypsies.

I will travel to Cordoba, Granada, Majorca, and Valencia. I have no interest in Barcelona or Madrid. Or even Seville.

He is there, somewhere.

He was in Cordoba for three days. He wrote that there was a beautiful Moorish bridge spanning the Guadalquivir River.

Then he was in Majorca, which I saw from my map was an island. He wrote about the Sierra de Tramuntana, and about a Carthusian monastery. He wrote about a museum that contained letters from the writer George Sand to her lover, the composer Frédéric Chopin. What did the letters say, I asked him. But he never replied.

The next I heard from him, he was in Alcoy, for the annual fiesta.

And then he was in Granada and wrote about the River Darro.

And then I waited. And waited. And waited.

And there was nothing. Nothing. Nothing.

I thought he had probably run out of money, which was why he could no longer afford the internet cafés.

At one point, I even entertained the thought that he had been murdered. I imagined his body lying by the side of the road. I imagined a red rose blooming from his throat.

I didn't want him to die. Not, at least, until he had reached Segovia, because I so longed to read his descriptions of that ancient town.

But now I will never know Segovia. Unless I go there myself.

I will never see Romanesque churches. I will never see Gothic cathedrals. I will never see the Costa del Sol. I will never be able to sample the local *rioja*, which he once told me had the aftertaste of honey.

And then Casares, with its whitewashed houses. I will never see that town, as well.

Or the Rock of Gibraltar.

Never to know these places would be a tragedy.

I would like to travel. I would.

When I have arrived at Frigiliana, which I understand is a very beautiful town, overlooking the Costa del Sol, I will think of life, and flamenco, and sun. The white will hurt my eyes, and I will taste the fine local wine, which will float over my tongue, smooth as truth, lovely as honey.

– 0 –

APPETITES

When she was a girl, she ate crab, bitter melon, rice soup. She loved milkfish, which at that time was still abundant. The cook, who was as dear to her as her own mother, served her glutinous rice cakes, salmon cured with tamarind salt, grilled squid stuffed with chorizo, the meat of young coconuts.

When she was a toddler, Cook cut everything into tiny morsels so that the girl's mouth would not stretch and become wide and ugly. The girl ate only the sweetest pastries, the sweetest pickles, only the smallest and most tender eggplants: Cook herself grew these in a corner of the garden, which every summer sprouted with little trees with purple-tinged leaves.

She loved fried bananas, but they were bad for her complexion so Cook served them to her only once a month.

Later, the girl developed strange predilections: she would eat bamboo shoots, but only when cooked in milk; she would eat corn, but only if silk threads still clung to the infinitesimal spaces between the kernels; she hungered for taro leaves, but only when braised in a sauce made from roasted capsicum; she liked dishes cooked in vinegar and garlic, and soft noodles sautéed with pork hocks. To disguise the girl's increasingly sour breath, Cook served her bowls of coconut flakes sweetened with brown sugar.

Later still, the girl would demand that she only be served okra if it had been fried in a cast-iron skillet made to her exact specifications. Her squid must come encased in steamed rice cakes, her plantains boiled in the water in which she herself had bathed that morning.

She would suck the juice from raw shrimp shells, and demand that Cook stir her soup with a counter-clockwise motion of the left hand.

Cook grew weary.

The girl didn't notice.

She wanted more and more of the purple sweet yams that grew on the slopes of the volcano looming in the distance. She drank only water flavored with annatto. She began to crave food that was harder and harder to procure: the eggs of monitor lizards, at that time already hunted to near-extinction, the eyes of albino water buffalos.

Cook walked farther and farther.

One day, she walked so far that she lost her way and did not know how to go back again. She sank to her knees and wailed piteously, by an ocean whose water was of an indescribable warmth, where the fish had scales of strange iridescent hues.

The girl waited, refusing to eat until the cook returned.

The girl's mother, who herself was as thin as a sapling, as thin as a cane of bamboo, watched her daughter from the door of the bedroom, wringing her hands in lamentation at her daughter's strange ways. Already, she knew it was too late.

$$- 0 -$$

THE ELEPHANT

The elephant's hide was a beautiful, dark grey. It was young: little more than a baby. Zoo officials paid a small fortune to have the calf shipped from Sarawak, in the Malaysian archipelago.

The captain had been told that the elephant had a name. Its name was Pebbles.

The captain asked, Why Pebbles? The man who sold the captain the elephant shrugged and said, *My son. He is seven. He named the elephant.*

For over a week, the elephant's wild thrashings sent reverberations throughout the ship.

It threw itself against the walls of its container, again and again.

Sea monsters! the crew awoke thinking. We're all going to die!

Electric shocks proved the solution.

The rest of the journey was uneventful. Summer storms were few and scattered. From Sarawak the ship outfitted in Kuala Lumpur and then made it to Bali.

In Bali, the captain's wife came aboard. She was a surprisingly young woman, with lustrous black hair that she wore in a loose twist, displaying a long, elegant neck. After this, the men relaxed. A man in love was the best captain.

Finally, the ship reached its destination, San Diego. The captain was horrified by the discovery of long, angry scratches raking the elephant's sides. The underside of the elephant's trunk was peppered with cigarette burns.

"Who did this?" the captain roared. The captain's wife turned her head away. Her incomparably slender neck drooped, as if under the yoke of a terrible burden. The crew had been gathered on the deck. No one spoke. It was as if they all had been turned to stone.

The zoo abruptly cancelled the press releases.

Down in the hold, the elephant calf lunged and lunged, wildly crying, struggling with all its might. Nothing in the world, not the painful tears of the captain's wife, or the anger of the zoo officials, could adequately account for the captain's shame and his sense of the mission's futility.

– 0 –

THE WALKER

I like to walk. I usually start at 3 a.m., when it's nice and peaceful. The neighbors are all in bed, their curtains drawn.

On some streets, I smell dog piss. On others, I smell jasmine. One street, my favorite, is lined with rose bushes on both sides.

That's the street where Mr. Flores lives. We've hardly exchanged more than a few conversations over the years. Someone told me he was from the Philippines. That's where he goes every summer, with his blonde wife and their two boys. The house stays empty for a month or two. Then I see either him or his wife working on their front lawn. I wave, they wave back.

There's one thing about him that has stuck in my mind.

It was the day after the towers fell. We watched it on the news: the smoke, the dazed people wandering the streets with their faces and clothes covered in white dust. None of us could find words.

That night, one of the neighbors put a single candle on his driveway as a symbol of mourning, and the rest of us followed suit. One candle in each driveway, for blocks. I remember standing on the sidewalk that night, watching as the candles guttered in the wind.

That's when I started walking. It was maybe 2 a.m. when I walked down Mr. Flores's street. Nothing caught my attention. The next night, I was back, and this time, I had to stop and stare. On Mr. Flores's front lawn was a large screen. It was as big as one of those billboards you see lining 101 just west of the Bay Bridge.

The screen was lit with a glowing red 1. I shivered, though it wasn't cold. I wondered what the number stood for. I passed his house again the very next night. This time, the number glowing on the screen was 2. Each night after that, I walked past his house. The number on the screen always increased by one. The screen was marking time of some sort, I knew that, but no explanation came from Mr. Flores and I felt it would be wrong to ask.

I didn't know it then, but another person was also marking time, restlessly pacing the perimeters of a walled compound in Abbottabad.

Ten years after the towers fell, on a cool night in early May, a team of Navy seals sent by our 44th president breached the walls of the compound and killed Osama bin Laden. It was all over the news. When we heard, we crowded around the TV and whooped and cheered. I opened a bottle of 12-year-old Macallan that I'd been saving for my birthday.

It wasn't until almost a week later that my memory stirred. Something felt wrong. I worried the notion, over and over. Finally, on that night's walk, I realized the screen that used to be on Mr. Flores's front lawn was gone. I stopped in front of it and stared, not quite believing, but there was no escaping it: Mr. Flores's lawn was as peaceful and empty as it had been on the morning of September 11, 2001.

For a long time, I stood before the blank green square of my neighbor's lawn and stared. Then I circled the block and came back. I did that three times.

Mr. Flores's house is one of those low, ranch-type houses that used to be popular in the 1950s. At the far end of the yard, just in front of a large picture window, are masses of billowing red rhododendrons. The walk that leads to the front door is lined on both sides with lavender. I had loved this house for many years, loved the smell of the lavender and the baskets of red and purple geraniums that hung from the eaves.

I didn't know if I loved it more because of the countdown screen, or whether I loved the house in spite of it.

But that night, that night when I realized the screen was gone for good, I knew I didn't love the house any longer. The fragrant, deep red blooms of the roses next door, the roses that I'd been admiring only a few days ago, were no longer alluring. Now, for some reason, the deep red reminded me of funeral bouquets, whose overpowering sweetness always makes me feel faint.

~

At first, when I started doing this thing, this walking in the wee hours, my wife would wait up for me.

"Ed," she would say, almost as soon as I walked in the door. "I don't understand why you're doing this. What's troubling you?" Her gentle voice was sad.

I knew I loved her. I loved her more when she was anxious about me. So of course, I loved her to a much greater degree at 5 a.m., when the sun was just beginning to appear over the rooftops.

After five or six years, though, my wife gave up. Her heart, she said, couldn't take the strain. She said she had to sleep at a normal hour. She also moved her clothes out of our bedroom. Now she sleeps in the guest room on the first floor. Our two sons, Charlie and Michael, seem to have taken this in stride.

Both my sons attend private school. They have seen everything: been at parties where 45-year-old dads plied the high schoolers with beer or whiskey. When Charlie was a freshman, he saw Melissa, a girl he had a crush on, get so drunk she threw up in the host's bathroom and passed out. Seven boys crowded the bathroom, for almost an hour. Melissa never woke up.

She wasn't in school the next day. Or the next. Or the next. She was gone. No one missed her. No one remembered her. Except Charlie. He's a senior now, and I can count on the fingers of one hand the number of parties he's attended. He saved up his allowance, and set up a punching bag in the garage. I can hear him grunting against the bag, most nights. He won't tell me what's wrong.

~

My city is called Sequoia. Sometime in the past, there were stands of these trees covering the low hills of California. They must have been quite a sight when the first settlers came here. None of those giant trees remain. In their place are strip malls and suburbs, mile after mile of them, as far as the eye can see, and of course the grid of streets where I walk.

When I walk, I count off the intersections: Topaz, Jade, Ruby. Ruby has the nicest houses. At one end, the street slopes upwards. In the fall, when I'm driving home and the light hits the tree tops at a particular angle, I have to hold my breath: there's a blaze in those leaves. There's heat and mystery. Then, a few weeks later, the trees are bare, and everything shuts down again, and I feel as if I'm sleepwalking.

I don't know why, but all the neighbors on Ruby have only red roses. My wife tells me that there are different kinds of red roses. She shows me her gardening catalogs: there are Don Juans, and Mr. Lincolns, Playboys, and Starinas. And there's a kind called All Dressed Up, which is a shrub rose, and not, my wife says, very vigorous.

My wife orders roses from the catalogs. They arrive in long cardboard boxes, a bundle of twigs. She used to be able to dig the planting holes by herself, but in the last couple of years, she asks our sons to do it for her. They complain a lot about it. A girl who lives down the street comes by sometimes to watch and stare. My wife wants the holes a foot-and-a-half deep, at least, because our soil is hardpan clay and the roses don't grow well unless she mixes in stuff. It is hard work, this digging, and sometimes it takes my sons over an hour.

The girl down the street, whose name I don't remember, sometimes looks at me with her eyes narrowed, and I wonder what she thinks. I look right back at her. If I'm feeling mean, I'll start smoking. The smoke will waft over to her, and she'll give a little grimace—kids of her generation, they hate old people like me who have nicotine-stained teeth and fingernails. They're all healthy—until they get into a car accident or dive into a pool drunk or collapse from a heart defect no one even knew they had.

But me, I love the smell of cigarette smoke. It deadens me to other things. They say smoking will shorten my life by a decade, but I know it won't. Life's a crapshoot. My younger sister, younger than me by seven years—she never smoked. Not after she turned twenty. She still developed emphysema. She got weaker, weaker, weaker. In the last year of her life, she couldn't go anywhere without a tank of oxygen and a tube running out of her nose. Her kids were ashamed to be seen with her. Her skin got leathery, old-looking, even though she was only forty-five. She died five years ago. Her husband married again, and now I hear he has a little boy.

Every single person I know is going to die. No exceptions. It sometimes paralyzes me, the thought. The neighbor's blonde twins, still in high school—in fifty, maybe sixty years, they'll be gone, to be replaced by other teenagers. And no one outside the twins' circle of family and friends will think anything of their absence.

How can others endure, I think. How? To think all this: my family, my wife and children, will one day be no more. They might leave behind traces, but so what? Perhaps my boys will have children, and perhaps those grandchildren will remember me. But in a few decades, even my grandsons will be replaced by people who will not regard me as a grandfather. They might not even know my name. The most I will be is a photograph in a picture frame.

Everywhere I look, there are people absorbed by what they are doing in the present, oblivious or indifferent to the fact that the future contains a non-commutable sentence.

I'm amazed that people can still summon happiness.

Who created this situation? Who hated people that much? Who?

The days outgrow one another. God is in the details. I think of bringing something to Mr. Flores: a six-pack of Pacifico and maybe some tomatoes from the garden. It's a Saturday, he should be home. I'll ring the bell. If there isn't an answer, I can see myself walking right in. Maybe he'll be sitting on the couch, watching TV, the TV whose blue glow I see most nights when I walk past. He'll look up. He'll be surprised. I don't think he'll be angry. He knows who I am.

I'll tell him all I've learned, the past ten years. I'll tell him how difficult it is, to fall in love with something only to have to let it go.

– 0 –

THE FUTURE

Against Sunshine's better judgement, she went to see a fortune teller. The fortune teller's name was Willow. The sign in front of her dilapidated house said RUNES, TAROT, PALM READINGS.

Afterward, the first person she thought to call was her husband.

The husband who disappeared almost a year ago. It was habit.

Both her children were away at college: the older, the girl, at a distance of almost two thousand miles. Sunshine lost track of her, this daughter, almost entirely in the last two years. Her daughter refused to go home for holidays, even for Christmas. Sunshine chided herself for this.

Samuel was studying in the University of Indiana at Bloomington. He hardly came home, either.

"You will enter a great forest," Willow said.

Sonny, Sunshine's husband, had worked almost two years for a start-up in San Ramon, almost thirty miles away. She last saw him just before 8 a.m., on a March morning, when he'd eased his blue Prius out of the garage. She stood at the door waving, as she always did. It was not a gesture of farewell, but a reminder. *You must come home to me.* The air, she remembered, had the gathering heat of a late spring day.

Sonny always told her she had too much energy. He'd say, *You're making yourself sick over this.* Then, How much sleep did you get last night?

She'd been averaging three hours a night for over twenty years. Amazingly, it didn't show on her face. Other women got eyebags.

Sunshine's face grew luminous. As if she really was a creature of dreams and darkness. She was made for them. She lived for them.

She began reading a new collection of short stories by a young Scottish woman. "Everywhere, glowworms shone with a green fire." The heroines in almost all the stories had green eyes and flame-red hair. She tried to picture such ethereal beings. On the top of a new page of her journal, she wrote the words *Spell* and *Fantasy*.

She tried to remember the last time she had lain down beside Sonny in the bed they had bought just before their wedding. His scent wrapping around her. Musky, not a particularly appealing smell. But so him. Why had he disappeared? A cousin asked, "Did he have a girlfriend?"

They found his body in a washed-out gully of a stream two hundred miles north. Throat slashed, his belt and his wallet missing. He had always been such a careful man.

She read, from the Scottish writer: *she had stopped to wash her face in a woodland pond, without knowing where she was bound.*

Willow had told her: "Never fear. You will become an old woman." Well, what did she know.

– 0 –

SAMAEL

Angels, according to my research, are supposed to be sexually ambivalent. The one I live with is emphatically male. Can angels switch genders, from male to female, or to somewhere in between, according to the current project? How did I get to be the current project, anyway?

One day, I came home with irises.

Samael's voice roused me from a daydream. "Are those for me?" he asked.

"Newp," I said. "These are for *me*."

I took a deep breath. I grabbed an empty glass from the kitchen, filled it halfway with water, and popped the flowers in. I decided that this was as good a time as any to have the talk. I'd done some research. "There are nine classes of angel. Which one are you?" I asked.

Samael turned to face me. He didn't say anything, just flashed me a blinding smile. For a minute I wondered if he'd take off: flap his invisible angel wings and take off like a spaceship.

I refused to be deterred. "Cherubim?"

He snorted.

"Seraphim?"

"Why do you need to know?"

"I just do. Archangel?"

"Stop it," he said.

"Where's your flaming sword? Does the name Gabriel ring a bell?"

He sighed. "Angels are messengers. Why would we need flaming swords?"

"I need you to convince me you're not just a homeless man taking advantage of my kindness."

Samael's eyes went wide. "I would never take advantage of you."

"Right," I said. I picked up my knapsack and slung it over one shoulder.

"Oh, are you leaving? Was it something I said?"

I shook my head. I didn't bother replying, just walked out the door.

I stopped going to mass as soon as I started at UC Berkeley. This didn't change, even after meeting Samael. But, one morning, I found myself wandering into a bookstore on Telegraph, the one run by the Sisters of Saint Paul.

Trying to be unobtrusive, I ignored the glass display cases, with their rosaries and reliquaries, and headed straight for the bookshelves that lined the far wall.

I was barely in there five minutes when the woman behind the counter said, "I see you're interested in angels."

I knew right away she was Filipina, like me. But she didn't switch to Tagalog, like most of the older Filipina women I'd met. I was grateful for that. My Tagalog was elementary, to say the least.

I ended up walking out with a slim paperback called *Essential Guide to Angels*.

I stuck a bowl of ramen in the microwave and was just about to start reading when Samael caught me.

He smirked and said, "What did you expect? I let you see me and now you're *disappointed?*"

I'm *that* obvious?

"I don't know what I expected," I said, annoyed. "A chubby baby with wings? Flitting against a blue sky?"

Or, I thought, something brilliant, fiery. The angel Gabriel coming to Mary.

Samael had bright blue eyes that he tried to hide behind black Ray Bans, and even though he'd taken to wearing an Oakland A's baseball cap pulled low over his brow, a stray curl always poked out and I had a hard time restraining myself from tucking it behind his ear.

"I'm sorry. I'm conventionally handsome. So what?" He sat down and picked up an apple from a bowl on the kitchen table. "I'm hungry. Feed me."

"You took an apple," I said.

"Not enough," he said. "A gammon joint. With apple and whiskey sauce."

"Potatoes over there. In the basket by the corner."

"Got any rapeseed oil? To fry with?"

"Sorry. What are you good for anyway? All you do is eat. It would be great if you acquired some skills. I could use someone who could help me pay the rent."

He shrugged and gave me a rueful smile.

"Why are you really here? I'm a student. I barely have enough for me. And, I'm sorry, I'm down to my last four eggs. You can't have any of those."

Again, he didn't answer, only turned his face away, as if he was hurt.

He'd been living with me for two weeks now. I'd been watching him from every angle, and at different times of the day. He ate a lot, but so far everything was fine. I knew I could go weeks, months like this.

I asked him if he'd been with me since birth. He smiled and said, "What do you think?"

I tried again: "Have I been baptized?"

He rolled his eyes.

"Tell me," I insisted.

"What are you doing, Lauren?"

"Research."

"What are you *really* doing?"

I scowled and crossed my arms over my chest.

"Of course you've been baptized. Filipinos always baptize their babies."

Right then I wanted to say, "You don't know anything about Filipinos." But I didn't.

He winked at me.

Gimme a break, I wanted to say. My parents kept statues of the Blessed Virgin in each room of the house, and even in the garden. But I was never a religious person. I associated this behavior with the Philippines and it was just one more way I was different from them.

I walked out of the room. The next time I saw him, he was eating tuna straight out of a can I didn't even know I had. "All right," he said, without looking up. "Since you have the relentlessness of a spider monkey, I will tell you something about myself: I was born in the Garden of Eden."

"Oh my God," I said. "Are you being serious right now?"

Do you know what it feels like to catch an angel going through your closet? Let me tell you, your heart races. He said he was looking for something, I forget what.

I looked at him. Clearly male. Great – ass. That flat stomach. And not at all squeamish about walking around naked.

The truth is, if I had that body, I'd probably be walking around naked, too.

Once, he caught me looking.

"Am I distracting you, Lauren?"

I had never seen another man naked. So, yes, I was distracted. But I was in college now, attending Berkeley, and so I didn't want to make a big deal about it. It might even help me, say I ever got to the stage where a boy I liked and I . . . newp, there I was, getting ahead of myself again. I had the social life of a slug. This might be the only naked man I'd see in college. I might as well enjoy it.

The way I acquired Samael was: he fell.

That's right: he fell from a great height, right into the dumpster below my window. It just so happened I was staring out the window, starting in on my first coffee of the day. I saw a blur. Then heard a terrifying THUMP. I screamed, "Jesus," spilled coffee all over myself, and ran to the window.

"I'm fine," Samael said, getting up. He looked curiously around him. "Where am I?"

I should have screamed.

I wondered if I should help find Samael – that's his name, Sa-MAH-el – a mate. A fellow angel. Preferably someone who shared his porn addiction and his fondness for beer.

As if I didn't have enough on my mind already. Like studying. And stopping my parents from sending copies of my Berkeley acceptance letter to all the relatives, even the ones in the Philippines we hadn't heard from in years.

He got distant when I told him it was my turn to host study group. For a moment, I wondered if things would get thrown, like when Grumpy Michael lived here. To tell you the truth, I had no idea how to deal with an angel's moods. After years spent binge-watching *True Blood* and *Vampire Diaries*, I felt very well equipped to deal with two things: curses and fangs. I even knew what to do if called upon to perform an exorcism: I kept a crucifix on my nightstand, a bottle of holy water in my desk drawer. But angel hissy fits? Not so much.

He said he could contribute snacks.

"How?" I said. "You don't have any money."

"That is not your concern, Lauren. I said I could provide snacks. Trust me on this."

"What kind of snacks?"

"Roast walnuts, peeled and chopped. . .

I waved my hand: "STOP! I'll get nachos."

"Nachos?" His mouth fell open. "Is that a thing?" He went straight to my laptop and googled 'Nachos.' After a few moments, he turned to look at me. "These are not good for you, Lauren."

I got home from the store. Samael helped me unbag my groceries. He pulled out the bottles one by one and examined them carefully before setting them on the counter: "Bourbon, vodka, gin, rum, aquavit . . . is this all just for study group?"

"Umm. Yeah."

"No beer."

I crossed my arms. "Beer is for wimps."

He stared. Stared, stared, stared. Ever had an angel stare at you? Yes, exactly.

He said it was fine if I kicked him out, he'd always respect my choices. He'd be like one of those angels who drives vans and does Hollywood tours (does he even know how to drive, I wonder?). Or he'd find a shelter. Hopefully he'd never become the target of shakedowns. I could think of one other occupation for him, but I decided not to say anything.

My phone rang at 5:45. It was Maxine. Meanwhile, Samael had disappeared. The group would arrive in fifteen minutes and I had no idea where Samael was. I couldn't focus. I had to find him.

Voice-in-my-head Samael: Why are you so distracted by this and that?

Samael walked in the door. To his credit, he had clothes on . . . a white T-shirt, and cowboy boots. I'd heard stories from the time when public nudity . . . But those times were long gone."

He bore a box and a huge grin

"What did you get?" I asked.

"Krispy Kreme doughnuts."

"How much were they?"

"Nothing. I stole them."

I snorted and opened the box. "There's one missing."

"Oh." He had the decency to blush. "That. Umm . . . "

"It's okay," I said. "Just sit down somewhere and try to look busy, all right?"

"I want you to know," Samael said, looking very earnestly into my eyes, "that I will pay you back every dollar that you spent feeding me, and I know I should chip in for the rent. There's a McDonald's down the street looking for a fry cook . . . "

"Seriously?"

He looked at me brightly and nodded.

Briefly, I closed my eyes, trying to picture him there in one of those triangular paper hats.

He would be absolute crap. He'd engage the customers in conversation and forget to hand them their orders. Plus, I was pretty sure he couldn't deal with oil splatter. I waved him off. "It's my pleasure, truly," I said. It didn't even feel like a whole lie.

The first of the group to arrive were Kyle and Edgar. It figured. They both liked competing for my attention, even though neither of them truly liked me. It was exhausting. Given the fact that they were both Asian, I wondered if their parents told them they had to find a "nice" girl, someone who could cook, and sew. I couldn't do either of those things, but I'm Filipina so they must have assumed that I could.

Kyle was from Monterey Park, but his parents were from the Philippines, like mine. Edgar was from Hong Kong. They were technically sophomores but they waited out a year because of covid. Me? I was born right here in the Bay Area, in a house on Tipperary Street in South San Francisco. I was the first person in my large extended family to get accepted to a UC. My parents even framed my acceptance letter. I spent most of last year taking classes online. My parents were thrilled to have another year with me.

Kyle and Edward stopped dead when they saw Samael. Samael took up so much space, just sitting there cross-legged in front of the TV (What was he watching? Oh, the news. I sighed with relief). Samael waved nonchalantly at them and then went back to watching the news.

K & E made urgent gestures for me to step into the hallway. "What is that huge, blonde man doing in your living room? Did you go on OK Cupid?"

"Knock it off," I said. I walked back into the apartment and they followed.

Maxine arrived. She stared at Samael with great, big, poodle eyes. Then Jean and Russell, holding hands (*When* did they start dating?) My living room felt stifling, the way a bus feels when it's too full.

"Rina can't make it," Jean says. "Asthma attack."

"Oh," I said. Then before I could say anything more, Samael piped up, "That's too bad."

Every head in the room swiveled around. "I'm Samael," he said. "I'm her—"

"Cousin," I said, quickly. "Second cousin. From Seattle. Just drove down."

"Pleased to meet you, Samuel," Maxine said, still with the big, poodle eyes.

"Sa-MAH-el, not Sa-MOO-el," Samael said, grinning. Why did angels have to have perfect teeth? And dimples. It wasn't fair. And by the way, where did he keep his wings? Did they fold into his back, or—?

He jumped up — I swear, the floor shook. He headed to the kitchen. When he came back out, he was balancing at least three plates in his huge hands, a doughnut on each plate. "Refreshments!" he said, with his most winning smile.

"Uh, thanks?" Maxine said. "Care to join us?"

"No, thank you," Samael said. "I have stuff to do." Then he twirled out the door.

As soon as he was gone, Maxine elbowed me in the ribs. "That's not your cousin. How'd you meet him? OK Cupid?"

Samael didn't come back until late, really late. I lay stretched across my bed, too wasted to take off my clothes. Still, I knew exactly when he got back, because I felt him standing at the door to my room, just looking.

"Was it good?" he asked.

"Wha --- ? Shtu-dee group?" I shook my head, back and forth. Which was harder to do than I'd thought, especially lying down. "We shtu-dee'd. Yeah. Good." Burp.

He stared at me more intensely than usual. "Are you unhappy, Lauren?" he asked.

Now he had my attention. I got up on one elbow and stared at him. "Nooooo. No, you don't get to ask that. You—you're not . . . my parent. Fuck." I loved the way that word sounded. I tried it out a few more times. "Fuck. Fuck. Fuck."

"I'm your friend."

"You? How can you be my friend? You're—whatever you are."

"I can be a friend. If you want. If you need one."

I thought about it for a moment. "No."

I fell back on the bed and put an arm over my eyes. "Where were you?"

"Around. I'm always around. Lauren, I can tell you're sad."

"Sa-MAH-el, are you really an angel?"

"Of course I am."

"Show me your wings."

"What?"

"I want to see you fly. I won't be sad if I can see that. Actually, can I fly, too? Can you teach me?"

He shook his head. "I'm sorry, I can't. When I assumed human form, I lost the ability to fly."

"I want to see you fly."

He shook his head. He bit his lip. "Here." He came forward and put something small but unbelievably heavy in my hand. I cracked my eyes open.

"What is this?"

"It's a lightning bolt. Well, not a real one. But this one's from Dharamsala."

"What am I going to do with this?"

"It'll give you power. Or make you feel powerful, anyway. Give it a squeeze. Go on. Try it."

I looked at the thing in my hand. "Is this really from Dharamsala?"

Samael nodded.

The thing was shaped like a barbell. It had an iridescent green patina.

"When were you there?"

He smiled. "A long, long time ago."

"Did you have to save someone?"

"In a manner of speaking."

"How come you never say it?" I asked. "I keep expecting to hear you say 'Go in peace' or something. Isn't that what every angel learns to say, first thing?"

Samael shook his head. "You know nothing about angels, Lauren. You let yourself get distracted by this and that."

"What?" My face flamed. He smirked.

"What is it you seek, Lauren?"

"Nothing. I'm happy as I am."

"That's not true."

"OK, how about this? I want to fall in love. No — to have someone fall in love with *me*."

"And you seek this? Truly?"

"No, not truly." I looked away from him. "How can I think of love? I look around me and all I see is terror and desolation."

"This world view of yours. I don't like it. Not for you."

I sat up. "How can I be happy in this land of the shadow of death?"

"You are losing someone close to you? Is that it?"

I ignored him. Samael shook his head. "You are such a mystery, Lauren."

My face flamed. "What? How am I a mystery?"

He gave me a smirk. Samael shook his head. "You know nothing about angels, Lauren. For one thing, you didn't think angels ate meat. Or that we knew anything about sex."

He gave me a smirk. "It's all right. I'm celibate. Not all of us are, though."

I wanted to scream. Samael was beautiful. He had just the right amount of down on his forearms, his shoulder bones had an elegant simplicity, and his hips were slender as a swimmer's. He was tall, but not preposterously so. Not for the first time, I thought of kicking him out.

The week before finals, I hosted study group again. Samael sat just outside our circle, listening intently, a look of curiosity in his eyes. But he didn't make a sound, and pretty soon everyone ignored him, too busy reviewing what we thought was going to be in the finals.

After everyone left, I went to my room, lay on my bed, and stared at the ceiling. *What was I going to do?*

By then, I knew a bit more about angels. I knew that there were a total of 301,655,722 angels, divided into heavenly legions. A heavenly legion had 6,666 angels. Angels spoke to each other by way of interior speech. They could move instantly from place to place. They existed in a state of eternal joy, but wept at the crucifixion and still grieved for the sins of man.

Samael and I hardly spoke, after. I was too busy studying. I worried most about my Anthropology class under Professor Nesmith. I was flailing under mountains of arcana: Market Systems in Rural China. The Long Reach of the Cultural Revolution.

I had known the course was over my head, but I took it anyway. And then, when I knew I was headed straight for a B, I should have dropped. But I didn't. I gave an oral report, wrote a lot of stuff on the blackboard, and when I turned around to face the class, Professor Nesmith was smiling. That's why I didn't drop. Stupid.

Samael flitted about, trying his best to be unobtrusive.

A few days later, I came home from the library and walked into . . . a grotto. There were tiny blue lights everywhere: on the kitchen counter, along the bookcase, even on top of the refrigerator. It reminded me of Capri, of the one time my father had taken us on vacation. I was eleven. I wanted to see the Blue Grotto but my father said no, tours to there were expensive. So instead, I looked it up online. I imagined myself entering the cave.

"Merry Christmas!" Samael said. He came and stood right in front of me. "Do you like it?" he asked, biting his lip.

"I don't like it," I said, and watched him flinch. "I love it."

He opened his arms. Christ, I thought.

Whereas before Samael moved in, I had dreams — bright, technicolor dreams in which the occasional boy featured, and from which I would wake feeling a little angry at myself — after Samael, my life felt very full and I was not chasing anybody, not even in my subconscious.

I can't tell you exactly how it happened, but sometime during those weeks after I met Samael, I met someone. He was the guy who always sat on the purple bean bag right next to the reference desk. I did the staring thing and after a bit, he looked up. That's the thing with the stare, it works every time. It's the one thing I've learned to do to perfection. God knows I'd had plenty of practice, living with Samael.

He'd been frowning at his book, but when he lifted his face and saw me, he began to grin. As if I was someone he recognized, had even been waiting for. Had he been watching me, too?

I had never fallen in love before. Love, I'd thought, was not for the likes of someone like me. I was going to be something great but practical. Love, if it happened at all, would be a side thing.

His name was Phil, and he was a guy of few words. He never gave me flowers. Every time we went to his place, I asked myself if this was what love felt like.

During one of our many conversations, Samael told me I had to give myself a chance to see myself as a hero. "You are so brave," he said. "You go through life believing that all you have is yourself."

Samael didn't understand; I didn't want that for myself. I didn't care about being a hero. When I met Phil, that day in the library, I was ready. Or maybe I was just ready for change. Maybe I was tired of being lonely.

Samael was quiet when I got home. I realized that I didn't know how he spent his time. I should've asked, but I really wasn't interested. Usually, when I got home, he was sitting down. Sometimes on the bar stool in the kitchen. Other times, on the couch. I caught him watching porn once. His face had a sad look. After that, I only ever saw him watching CNN. "Why?" I asked him once. He paused as if thinking. Then he said, "It's nice. It's comforting." On the other hand, he could just have been preparing for his next assignment.

That day, the day I met Phil, Samael was quiet. I was quiet, too. I wanted to fantasize about me and Phil in the purple bean bag chair. Phil's hair had the perfect degree of flop, and his arms looked strong. He had blue eyes; they reminded me a little of someone.

Finally, Samael said: "I should be leaving soon, Lauren."

My eyebrows rose but I didn't say anything.

Samael continued, "I have another assignment."

"Oh?" I said. "Where?"

"Berlin," Samael said, and added, facetiously, "which is in Germany."

And for the first time, I was just a little sad. "Who is she?" I asked.

"Not a she," Samael said. "He needs help."

"So you only go where people need help?"

"Yes."

"But I didn't need any help."

"You did."

"No, I didn't."

Samael said, "I will not argue with you, Lauren." Then he turned to face me. His eyes, which I used to think were an intense blue, were actually not. They were a dark, dark, dark green.

"Didn't you tell me once that you wanted to fall in love, Lauren?" he asked.

"I lied."

"You do want to fall in love."

"What makes you say that?

"I can tell."

This was another of our "we stare at the point, and the point stares back" moments.

I asked him how soon he would be leaving, and he said, "Tomorrow."

That shook me. Tomorrow? I went to the fridge, grabbed a beer. I hadn't had to buy a beer since Samael came, he seemed to like Tsingtao best.

"How are you going to get to Germany?" I asked, after taking a long pull.

"I will get there, that is not your concern."

"You're flying. Flying on your angel wings. Ha. Ha."

"Stop this, Lauren."

I stared at something above his head. *Damn.* I swallowed. "You don't need me to drive you to the airport?"

"No."

I tried to imagine Samael moving around in a city I knew only from photographs. Samael speaking German. "Will I ever see you again?" I asked.

"Probably not."

I was quiet. "Lauren," he said, looking intently at me. "You are going to be okay."

The next morning, when I went to the kitchen to make coffee, I felt it right away. Samael wasn't on the couch, where he usually was when I awoke. I ran to the window overlooking the dumpster. The lid of the dumpster was closed. The street was just a street.

I backed away from the window. I didn't bother looking for him, I just knew.

I imagined Samael hurtling through the sky, his powerful wings extended. Would he miss me?

I missed him. I didn't realize it right away. I was a bit distracted. First, there was the flirting and then the sleeping with the boy I first saw on the purple bean bag chair. He was my first. Even though we wouldn't last, I was learning things.

One night, Phil started telling me about his family, and how he really wanted me to meet them on Thanksgiving. I got a flash, an image. *Samael!* I thought. *Are you all right? Are you really in Berlin? I'm sorry I never got to see your wings.*

I saw his face: it was very blurred, but I knew it was him. He still had the softest, kindest eyes.

Can angels die? I tried mental telepathy: *I hope you're all right, Samael. Wherever you are.* I listened carefully for the beat of invisible wings, for the slightest displacement of air. I placed my hands together, palm to palm, the way my parents did when they prayed.

My study group was very concerned the next time we met at my place. They were hoping to see Samael.

"He's back home," I said. "He was just visiting."

"That's too bad," Maxine said, and winked.

We opened our beers.

I'm an Unbeliever; but I still read every page of *The Essential Guide to Angels*.

Samael: alternatively Smal, Smil, Samil, or Samiel, an angel in Talmudic or post-Talmudic lore. He is believed to be the father of Cain, as well as the husband of Lilith. He is sometimes identified as a fallen angel. He also fills the role of the Angel of Death.

That gave me pause. The Angel of Death? Samael as the Angel of Death? No, he couldn't be.

It was unusually cold that fall, and I couldn't stop thinking of Berlin.

I longed to be surrounded by certainties. I decided to see my parents.

The house was small and gloomy. Had my room always been that tiny? Despite the fact that it was just my parents at home, the fridge and freezer were full.

"Is everything all right?" my mom asked, her forehead creased in concern.

"Yes," I lied.

"Go to your room and lie down," my mom said. "I'll bring you some ginger tea."

I obeyed, but how could I tell her? I missed him so much. Somehow, he had clawed his way into my heart.

I found myself staring at the painting of the Virgin on the wall opposite. It had hung there at least ten years. Blood trickled from her eyes.

I started to cry. My mom must have heard me. She rushed into the room. "Something's happened. You don't have to tell me." My father followed. He climbed into my bed from the other side. "You don't have to tell us," he said, over and over, "unless it'll make you feel better."

I was sorry for making them worry so much. I was such a coward. I wiped my tears away and tried smiling. I felt both of them relax.

"You've got the whole world in your hands," my father said. The way he said it, it was as if he was begging. Begging me to be okay.

I knew I had to be okay, for them. I nodded and said, "Yes."

− 0 −

DON ALFREDO & JOSE RIZAL

She hands me a story and says, You must read it, it is something about our great-grandfather.

I look at my cousin's earnest face, the planes of her cheeks, smooth and round as my mother's. My mother! Reigning beauty of her day, gone these many years, but when I look at my cousin I see her again. I see her tall Castilian nose, the dark fringe of lashes around her large brown eyes. "How like Teresita she is!" everyone used to say, of my cousin. I would bow my head, as if in humble obeisance to this beauty.

I open her manuscript and read the words:

Jose Rizal's Oil Lamp

But what does this have to do with *us*, with our great-grandfather, I say.

Our great-grandfather, Alfredo Buencamino, was a governor of the province of Albay in the last decade of the nineteenth century. The family had wanted me to write his story for a long time. There was a college named after him in a small town there. And all of us cousins had pictures of the man, dressed in *mestizo* finery—the same exact picture, showing a man with a luxuriant mustache, right hand resting on his barrel chest—hanging in our homes.

I did, in fact, begin to write this story, but there were things I discovered about my great-grandfather that bothered me. I discovered that he had more than one wife, the youngest a girl of 14. I discovered that he was uncommonly cruel. He tried his best to hide the fact that there was a strain of *indio* blood in his family, and he would beat his darker-colored servants mercilessly. He died mysteriously, perhaps a victim of poisoning.

You see, my cousin says, gesturing to the manuscript, we are related to the National Hero of the Philippines, Jose Rizal. The one who was shot by a firing squad in Luneta Park, in 1896.

Read it, she urges me. The story is true. And because something in her voice—something about the timbre, the slight tremor of her last words—touches me, I do look down at the pages in my hands, pages I hold lightly, uneasily, in my fingers, and read:

As Jose Rizal was lined up before the Spanish firing squad, labeled renegade and underground solidarity worker, George Dewey entered Manila Bay.

George Dewey. I would always think of him in connection with the man who had invented the Dewey decimal system, but this was not that man. This Dewey was an Admiral, an adventurer with dreams of empire, who entered Manila Bay in 1898 on a great American battleship, guns pointing at the crumbling embankment of Manila's old walled city, Intramuros.

I picture the blue water of the bay, the panic of the few Spanish soldiers watching on the gray stone battlements.

The residents of the city are sleeping peacefully, their breath rising in stagnant clouds over their heads as they lie beneath the mosquito nets draped over their mahogany four-posters. The dogs sniff in the lanes, the pigs root in the backyards. Roosters crow from various parts of the slumbering city.

Six o'clock in the morning but already the day is hot, the sun's heat falling like shards on the still-empty streets.

While the guns fire on the crippled Spanish fleet, demolishing it and killing 200 Spanish soldiers, Dewey is having a leisurely breakfast that lasts, if his servants are to be believed, from 7:30

a.m., when firing commences, to 11:15, when the white flag is hoisted over the old walls of Intramuros.

In Fort Santiago, the morning of his execution, Jose Rizal gave his personal belongings to his mother and his sister.

Give this oil lamp to Don Alfredo Buencamino, he instructed the women. A crumpled piece of paper lay inside. On that paper was his last farewell to the Filipino people, "Mi Ultimo Adios."

My cousin is speaking again, her voice low and urgent: The Spanish Guards came to Don Alfredo's home in the morning. They demanded the oil lamp. Lolo Bito handed it to them saying, Rizal left his oil lamp; you can have it. There is no wick, no oil in it. It does not work. It is empty.

Her voice begins ever so slightly to rise: *Mi Ultimo Adios*, the poem, Don Alfredo had already memorized it. He memorized the poem and destroyed the piece of paper. And as Dewey and the Americans entered Manila, the first thing Lolo Bito did was record the poem. And this is how Lolo preserved Jose Rizal's last words.

She stops and gazes at me. I read in that look a challenge.

But this is not true, I say. Don Alfredo never befriended Jose Rizal.

Moreover, I tell her, Jose Rizal was executed in 1896, and George Dewey did not enter Manila Bay until two years later.

My cousin's face assumes a petulant expression. Closed inward, the Asian cast of her eyes became more evident.

Tita Berna told me this story, she says. It's true.

Tita Berna! The crazy old woman who fought with my mother, all those many years ago. It was a silly quarrel, as most of our family disagreements are.

I thought she lived in Seattle, I say.

She does, my cousin says. I've been driving up there for the last couple of months. She tells me her stories and I tape them.

Look, I say, rising hastily and heading for my bookshelves. I have rows of books of Philippine history: Arcilla's, which had been my first history book, bought from Alemar's when I was still in convent school. A number of early books by William Henry Scott, when I had discovered Sagada and the beauty of its dark skies. Autobiographies by prominent Filipino public servants—de la Costa, Zulueta. Standard histories by Agoncillo, Zaide. I was always reading, and the history of the country I had left twenty years ago was never very far from my thoughts.

I open a book and recite: In Fr. Demetillo's account of Rizal's execution, Rizal is waiting by his cot when the soldiers come. His room is empty. There is a sheet of paper on the table.

When I finish reading, I look up. She has turned away from me, towards the window. I note vaguely that a stiff breeze is blowing the colorful pennants lining the Embarcadero.

And here, another, I say. His own wife tells of how she took the paper from Rizal's own hand, the one with the famous words that begin, in Spanish, *Adios, Patria adorada, region del sol querida* . . .

Farewell, beloved Country, treasured region of the sun,
Pearl of the sea of the Orient, our lost Eden!
To you eagerly I surrender this sad and gloomy life;
And were it brighter, fresher, more florid,
Even then I'd give it to you, for your sake alone.

In fields of battle, deliriously fighting,
Others give you their lives, without doubt, without regret;
The place matters not: where there's cypress, laurel or lily,
On a plank or open field, in combat or cruel martyrdom,
It's all the same if the home or country asks.

I die when I see the sky has unfurled its colors,
And at last after a cloak of darkness announces the day;
If you need scarlet to tint your dawn,
Shed my blood, pour it as the moment comes,
And may it be gilded by a reflection of the heavens' newly-born light.

The man in the black frock coat sits hunched over a wooden table, and presses pen to paper. It is quiet in his dank little cell in the bowels of the old fort. I can hear the scratches his pen makes on the coarse paper. The sweat trickles down the back of his neck.

The man's eyes, like mine, like all of us, have an Asian cast. But his clothes are European. A tailor in Madrid made his coat, when he was a young student there. That was long, long ago— before Bonifacio, before the Cry of Balintawak, before the ripping of the *cedulas*. And his wife has brought it to him with tears, so that he can face the firing squad with dignity.

I don't know, my cousin said. Tita Berna isn't crazy.

I want to retort, but something in the stoop of my cousin's back stops me.

Standing against the plate glass window, I marvel at the thin outline of her. The legs bronzed from surfing on Capistrano beach. Her hair streaked by the California sun. I think about her ex-husband, who left her for a kindergarten teacher while they were both waiting tables at the Captain's Bar in downtown Ensenada. Was that last year, or the year before? Time—the past—tunnels its way into our hearts, there is no way of knowing where all of this will end.

Her husband's name was Lou, he was tall and wore his blonde hair slicked back. The pair of them went surfing and I used to marvel, watching them, at their youth, their twin beauty. They had a child, one lovely daughter. They named her Elena. Counting backwards quickly, I decide she must be two or three now. I have never seen this child, though my cousin has sent me two—yes, I am sure just the two—pictures, once a year at Christmas.

Why does it matter? I ask now. That our great-great grandfather knew Rizal.

I studied it in school, she says. I took a course from a professor who had studied Rizal and the Philippine Revolution. After a pause, she adds, Father Reilly.

I'm happy that you did, I say. All young people should know about our history.

But this is different, she says. This is about our *family*.

I still can't see her face. I want to say, suddenly, Goddamnit, don't you turn away from me.

We have what psychologists might call a rather dysfunctional family. In fact, many of us do not even speak to each other anymore. We have Don Alfredo's picture in our homes, but we don't speak to each other.

We grew up hearing tales about Tita Erma's fights with her husband over money. When her youngest was 13, she ran off with a rich *haciendero* from Bacolod, leaving her husband and their three daughters. Naturally, he blamed our family. None of us can even visit to see the girls.

Manong Tony likes to gamble. Once he lost close to two million pesos at Marapara. His wife had a nervous breakdown. Now, my friends in Manila tell me they see her from time to time, laughing in bars with strange men, her face tightened, its sharp contours giving off brittle accents.

My sister, Fe, is much older than me. Diabetic, she moved back to Manila when she became too frail to take her regular afternoon walk around the block. She lives with my younger brother, who keeps her in a room of the house and tries to pretend she isn't there.

And as for the rest, my other cousins, one lives in Miami, in a long white house with a lap pool and security guards. The other lives a few hours north of me, in Santa Maria. I haven't seen either of them in over seven years. The last time I visited the Miami cousin, he talked endlessly about women in front of his wife. His wife sat meekly, her head bowed. The cousin in Santa Maria has a drinking problem. It is difficult for me to visit and see the way he mixes his vodka with orange juice, so early in the morning.

I'm taking writing courses, my cousin says. I want to be a writer someday. She adds, so softly I almost don't catch it, like you.

She picks up a knife. Smooth-edged, the one I had just been using to slice up tomatoes for a salad. She runs it across the tanned skin of her forearm, back and forth. I had sharpened it just a few hours ago. Little welts of blood begin to rise around her elbow.

Don't don't don't don't, I say.

You think I'm crazy, she says. For thinking that about Rizal. About our great-great grandfather.

I do not think you are crazy, I say. I shake my head. A pressure builds behind my eyes. My vision begins to blur. I know, it means a lot to you.

Oh well, she says.

She puts down the knife. She yanks a paper towel from the roll on the counter and presses it against her forearm. The blood makes red stripes on the white sheet. I can't tear my eyes away.

I'm sorry, I've worried you, she says. I am all right. I'll go now.

Wait! I say. Can I offer you something, something to eat. Stay and have *merienda*. I have these biscuits—*panaderia de molo*. Someone brought them from the Philippines, only a few days ago. They are so fresh! Let's have some down by the beach.

No, no, she says. I have to go.

How long have you been doing that?

Doing what? she says, and laughs. The paper towels are discarded on the counter now. I can still see the marks on her forearms, blood beginning to well up again, slowly.

Then I say, I'm sorry. I didn't know you knew about Jose Rizal.

It's fine, she says, still laughing. It's all right. What do I know, after all? I'm not like you, a university professor. All those articles you've published. The one on "The Second Colonization"? That was good.

But I really know nothing, I say. Nothing that truly matters. I've never been married. I don't have a child, like you.

She gives me a scornful look and leaves. I stare at the lines of the poem on the sheet of paper on the table. I see the short man in the black frock coat. He seems to be speaking to me, muttering something in a foreign tongue.

He is being led through a limestone tunnel, his arms tied behind his back. He emerges onto Bagumbayan field. His leather shoes slip on the marshy ground.

Soldiers are standing at the far end. They ready their rifles.

Now the man in the black frock coat is falling. Oh! He is falling. See, here come the ladies to dip white lace handkerchiefs in his blood. They will press the blood-stained cloth to their cheeks, murmuring. Their husbands frown but can do nothing. The women know the blood is sacred. They turn with a graceful movement of their wide skirts.

My eyes are blurry again. There is a catch somewhere at the back of my throat. I want to take the knife she left on the table and press it against the tender skin at the inner corner of my elbow, if only so that I can feel, just once, the sharp stab of pain, the ecstasy of blood.

– 0 –

SPINNING BY CANDLELIGHT

One late winter night, in a humble dwelling built of thick sod and grass, a wife sat spinning by candlelight. Her husband and son had gone to bed.

For a while, the wife listened to the North Wind blowing. Slowly, slowly, her eyes drifted shut and she began to dream about:

A sea creature with slashing teeth
Bracken and mountain moss
Her husband and little one
Her cheese and butter-keg
Her comb and wool cards
Her thread and distaff
Cow and fetter
Horse and traces
Harrows and hoard
Needles and loom
The Holy Book and a rowan branch

Who could explain why, at such an hour and in such weather, a knight walked in the door, bringing with him the dark.

The knight's eyes were shielded by the visor of his helmet. The wife saw that it was wet outside; drops were on his armor.

"God and Mary bless ye, good Sir," the wife cried. "Are ye lost?"

The knight shook his head. "Are ye?" he asked.

The wife was taken by surprise and could not answer. She raised one hand to tighten her shawl more closely around herself.

"Are you wanting supper, Sir," the wife said, gesturing to the rough-hewn table beside her. "You may sit." For politeness was always the best way to deal with strangers. Even though she had hardly any eggs to spare. And only days-old bread.

"No," the knight said. "I cannot stay."

"Where are you from?" the wife asked, surprising herself with her boldness.

"From across the sea," the knight said.

The woman thought the knight had something of a mad look about him. Something about the eyes. And his voice was not the voice of these parts.

But, really, how could one judge, when all she could see of him was that little slit in the visor of his helmet.

He extended a mailed hand, as if he expected to pull her back with him into the dark. Looking at the silvery fretwork of his glove, the woman thought of a sea creature, the one in her dream.

The woman quickly made the sign of the cross, put both hands behind her back, and shook her head.

The knight lowered his hand. His stance breathed disappointment.

"Each day you shall – " he began.

But the woman did not hear the rest of the sentence. She blinked, and the knight was gone. The door where he had stood was nothing but an empty black square. Above it, she saw the rowan branch she had hung there a short time before, merry with dark, green leaves. A hinge was loose and the door swung, back and forth, back and forth, blown by a high wind. The woman went to the door to make it fast, the bottom edge dragging across the dirt floor.

Though the knight had left only moments earlier, there was no trace of him, or of his horse. Where had he come from? Was he a true knight, or was he the devil?

She was greatly relieved to still be in her cottage, with the spinning wheel right behind her. She was tempted to tell her husband the story, but something she saw in his face the next morning made her think better on it. And she became even more confident in her decision when, mid-morning, a green plover came from the direction of the marshes, all alit, its voice crying of mystery.

The villagers made fun of her because she was born with only four fingers on one hand. Sometimes, standing at the shore with her husband, she tried to cast her mind into the briny deep. Her husband kept tight hold of her arm. He was thinking the same thing.

She took a long, shuddering breath, her knees trembling. But a small seed of discontent took root in her breast that night and, try as she might, she could never dislodge it.

The following winter, she had a new son. Unlike his older brother, this one liked to wander. He liked to feel the moor's springy heather underfoot. He ventured far, eating his mother's oat cakes and cheese, arriving home late and always enormously and insatiably hungry.

His father beat him, for the goat had not been milked, and the cock and hens had not been given their corn.

One day his father did a terrible thing, and the boy did not return.

"Oh!" cried the father. "He is carried away by the fairies, I am sure."

The wife sat spinning, wishing she had the courage to cross the wide sea.

One cold winter night, the wife sat dozing by the fire. So many years had passed that her hair had turned quite gray, and her heart felt like a lump of useless clay in her chest. Her husband and her eldest son had long since gone to bed. The spindle had fallen from her hand, and the fire had died down to a few embers.

She began dreaming of her boy, the one who loved to wander. She saw his young, clever face, and his mild eyes. His hair was still thick and brown, but shot through with streaks of silver. He turned a solemn face to her and said:

> Horse and traces
> Harrows and hoard
> Needles and loom
> The Holy Book and a rowan branch

Then the wife awoke. She looked at the door, expecting it to burst open at any moment. But it remained fast. She got up and flung it wide.

– 0 –

THE MARVELOUS ARCHIPELAGO

To His Majesty the King,

Our crew having paused for provisions in the Kingdom of Xian, and received a most hostile reception, we sailed farther south. We were overtaken by a storm and were driven off-course to a seemingly endless archipelago of islands, each of varying shape and size, some no wider than our ship's deck, others very large, with peaks that rival any in Europe. At length we succeeded in finding shelter on an island which we were told was called the Island of Fire, there being an active volcano at its very center. This was an excellent and large island, and having made shelter here, we befriended a few of the natives. We offered a prayer of thanks for our deliverance and were astonished to discover that the natives were familiar with the performance of the Divine Service. It happened to be the Feast of the Resurrection of Him who was our Salvation. After, the natives told us that they had a King, and that he came from the West.

They described him thus: Hair exceedingly black and falling to his shoulders. Two large golden earrings fastened to each ear. A cloth of silk draped across his hips and falling to his knees. A dagger tucked into his belt, the haft of which was long and full of gold, protected by a scabbard of carved wood. He had three spots of gold on every tooth, and he was perfumed with storax and benzoin.

Pieces of gold the size of coconuts are found by shifting the earth. All this gold is presented to the Island King. All the dishes of this King are of gold, and so are the walls of his home. The King is always very grandly decked out, and a more fine-looking man the islanders have never beheld.

They invited us to attend a procession, which they said was held every Easter (for they follow the Christian calendar). This procession, as far as we could make out, was led by someone holding a cross, and then by a number of islanders holding candles, and then by a group of children singing. Then followed the King, in ornamental vestments, who was shielded from the oppressive sun under a canopy supported by four maidens. The King himself joined in the singing and was said to have a very beautiful voice.

The destination of the procession was an altar erected in the heart of the forest, in front of which the procession paused for prayer. Then there was a great ringing of bells and a salvo of guns. Then the King blessed the forest, and all the islanders present.

After eight days, we proceeded to our destination. We met a group of Samal traders who told us that the island we had discovered was called Isla Encantada, for it never stayed in the same place for eight days together.

We tried forthwith to return to the Island, but despite many weeks of determined search, we never found it again.

Francisco Serrao, Explorer
January 1518

- 0 -

MAGELLAN'S MIRROR

The crew encountered the giant during the winter months they sheltered in the Philippine archipelago. He was described by the Spanish sailors as being "twelve or thirteen palmos" tall, which is to say, over eight feet. While the men watched from the ships, this singular individual danced and sang and leaped across the sand. Over his shoulders hung the pelt of an animal. Looking carefully at the pelt, the crew described it as having the head and ears of a mule, and a neck and body like those of a camel. On his feet he wore a pair of elaborate boots, made also from the skin of an animal, which added further to his already great height.

They were on the island of Butuan or Limasawa, it was difficult to ascertain which with any certainty: Antonio de Pigafetta, Italian navigator and ship's chronicler, was unclear in his journals.

It was the 3rd day of February in the year 1521. Of the date, there is no dispute.

Lured aboard, the giant was fed and given wine. When Magellan saw that the visitor was sated, he ordered his men to produce a mirror. The largest of these was an oval plaque of burnished metal, was kept in the captain's cabin at all times. Smaller ones were with the goods the crew would use as barter. It was the large one in his cabin that Magellan ordered the men to fetch.

When the burnished steel was set before him, the giant leaped back, grew agitated, shouted and in general exhibited all the attributes of profound terror. Not wishing to fall victim to the giant's violence, the crew quickly scattered. The mirror fell and a crack appeared at the bottom of the plaque, which many present took to be a most unpropitious omen. Some of the men drew their swords but Magellan bade them to desist. Stepping calmly forward, the captain picked up the mirror and threw his cloak over it. Whereupon the native's anger quickly subsided, and all were able to resume their seats at the table and continue their meal, although in absolute silence.

By the time the giant was taken back to shore, a number of other natives had collected on the beach. They had seen their tribesman being rowed to the black ship and seemed most anxious to know what had befallen him. As the longboat bearing their comrade approached the shore, more and more of these fantastical creatures emerged, so that eventually there were no less than a score of them on the beach, all watching the boat's approach in fear and apprehension.

We learn from the journals of the Pigafetta that some of these curious onlookers were women. These had teats, Pigafetta reported in some amazement, "half a cubit long." Furthermore, Pigafetta observed that while the men carried only their weapons, which consisted of long wooden spears, the women were burdened "like she-asses" with all manner of goods: pots, animal skins, beads, and feathered headdresses.

When the giant had been reunited with his companions, another very tall man came forward and offered the sailors food. Pigafetta has little to say about these offerings. In his journals he says generally that they were "good." *Bueno* is the word he used. In an aside, he also mentions that this man went by the name Casiburauen, and that he "was very ugly," *Feo*, Pigafetta wrote. *Muy feo*.

The crew named the first giant Enrique. Subsequently, they became hard-put to give names to all the tribesmen who made their acquaintance. They began to give them names that were variations of Enrique, so that some were Enri, others were Que, and some were Riq. And when they gestured to Enrique and mouthed his name, he had a way of looking, with his lips slightly parted, which made them wonder whether he suffered from some mental deficiency.

Relations between the Castilians and the tribe of giants continued cordial for some weeks. Then, one day, the captain led a group of sailors onshore to forage for food. They had been wandering in the jungle for some hours when they stumbled upon a deep pit, set well back from the beach. What aroused their suspicions was the obvious care which had been taken to conceal the pit's existence: the stones that had been laid carefully over the edge, the fresh thatch that lay on top of the neatly arranged stones. The men knew the natives to be of a generally lazy sort, their huts little more than hastily erected frames, and these good enough only for protection against light rain.

When the sailors pulled the thatch away from the stones, their consternation was great. In the shadowy depths could be discerned the outlines of a quantity of spears, each tipped with a tar-like substance the crew surmised might be poison. The men hastened back to the boats, and the dreadful find was the source of much frightened conjecture. From then on, Magellan ordered that the men keep to their boats, and when the giants next appeared on the beach, inveigling the men to disembark, the sailors implored Magellan to cast off. Magellan, however, was firm in his refusal: Winter was approaching, and the lands they were traversing were strange and new. They must winter here, he had already decided.

During the next week, no natives appeared on the shore. The beach was as empty as it had been on the first day before the crew had sighted Enrique. The sky had turned a cloudless blue and now the men began to remember the homes they had left behind, over a year earlier. The sun in Jaen and Valladolid was as cruel and merciless as the tropical sun, but now the men felt as if they had gone forth into a void. It would swallow them up; they feared dying in this wilderness. They cursed their leader under their breaths.

After the second week, some of the men took to leaving the boat at night, to hunt for the native women who they had seen on the first day. When Magellan discovered what the crew was doing, his punishment was swift and decisive: the guilty parties were chained to the mainmast and given no food or water for three days. During this time, the sailors saw fires lit on the beach, and gigantic figures walking to and fro. At the close of the third day, Magellan ordered the malefactors to be carried below deck, to have their piteously blistered skin tended to by the ship's doctor.

After the crew had endured this state of anxiety and apprehension for close to a month, a new and ugly rumor began to spread upon the gun-decks. Magellan, it was whispered, had made a pact with the King: to return only when the ships' holds were full of either gold or spice. The ship's pilot sank into a depressed torpor and Magellan could not rely on him to perform his usual duties. The ships creaked anxiously at their berths. A stench gradually arose from the lower deck, a stench of urine and sweat, of fear.

Hunger stalked the holds. But the men kept their heads down, fearing Magellan's terrible wrath. They mended their clothes as well as the ship's sails. They collected shrimp and boiled them in their iron kettles. They counted the number of shooting stars in the night sky. They pointed at the giant sea turtles making ponderous circuits around the ship. At night, one or the other of the men would begin a sullen, low, whistling. The tune would wind its way among the sleeping bodies. In these black, fearful nights, Magellan slept with his sword not far from his side. He had strange dreams.

In the middle of the fourth week, four of the giants suddenly re-appeared, gesticulating from the shore. The sailors shook their heads. The natives importuned them with tragic gestures. Finally, the tribesmen took out a canoe and began paddling towards the

Trinidad. Magellan ordered his men to welcome them warmly. The Castilians offered the visitors their fill of wine. Just as the men were sleepily dozing off, Magellan ordered his men to shackle them. By the time the natives realized what was happening, the ships had weighed anchor. What followed was a scene of great consternation as the giants made wild lunges at the crew, pulling with all their might against the shackles bolted to the deck, pulling so hard that the flesh of their legs soon became raw and bloody and, in the words of Pigafetta, "blowing and foaming at the mouth like bulls." At last, however, they succumbed to exhaustion and sank to the deck. Gradually, the true enormity of their fate seemed to impress itself upon them; their eyes glazed over with a kind of blank horror. As a group they set up a piteous moaning that continued without cease for three full days.

This was the only instance in which Pigafetta dared to confess that he found something less than honorable in the actions of his commander. He who had watched, impassive, when Magellan had ordered the mutinous Castilian captain, Hermenegildo Hilario, to be strangled in full view of all the men; who had dispassionately described the punishment meted to an officer caught sodomizing a cabin boy (The officer was drawn and quartered, with his own entrails set alight before his horrified, dying eyes), now referred, in his journal, to Magellan's "cunning deceit."

The sailors muttered curses as they gnawed sullenly on the hardtack. Everywhere, they saw portents: in the black bird that alighted one morning on the top of the forecastle, its red eyes blinking fiercely; in the dreams of the youngest sailor, who for a succession of nights dreamt of a huge animal, deer-like, crashing through undergrowth.

On the third day following the capture of the giants, a typhoon arose. The Victoria was tossed to her side as wave after wave washed over her deck. The men clung to the masts and beseeched Saint Nicholas for aid. The seas quieted, but for how long, no one knew.

One day, the captives suddenly ceased their lamentation. The cause for their silence was apparently this: they had not eaten in some days, and had observed how the crew regularly discovered and tossed overboard a great variety of rats, which creatures were considered a terrible nuisance on all ships, for it was impossible to be rid of them, and in the meantime they pilfered the ships' rations and consumed all that they could, leaving to the sailors only the hated hardtack. One of the captives had managed to seize a rat and promptly devoured it whole. His fellow captives were seized with envy and from then on outdid one another in competing to determine who among them showed the greatest skill and dexterity in trapping the rodents.

Observing how easily the natives' energies had been diverted, and how gleefully they laughed while holding the hissing rats up in the air, the crew surmised that the giants were no more than children, and from then on treated them accordingly.

For some weeks, the remaining ships continued southward without incident. They passed lovely, verdant islands, some no larger than a few meters across. The beaches were white and empty, the islands seemingly uninhabited. Perhaps out of boredom, Pigafetta set himself the task of understanding the captives' language. To this end, he began to create a dictionary, which at first consisted of the most elemental words: water, food. Gradually, however, he moved from the naming of objects to the naming of concepts such as hunger, desire, love. For hours he would sit with the giants, making notes and asking them to repeat certain words over and over. The word for *nose*, he ascertained, was the same as the word for *ear*. There was more than one word that stood for happiness. The word for mouth was the short, forceful *siam*. In his journal, Pigafetta wrote: "Their tongue is apparently monosyllabic; it seems to derive from the same Malay root as do the other Indo-

Pacific languages." Pigafetta wrote diligently; the giants stared at him placidly, with little understanding.

Sometimes the chronicler drew a cross on his paper and, pointing to it again and again, attempted to impart the concept of "God." The natives thought that he wanted them to repeat the word. "Deee," they said. "Deeee! Deeee!" Eventually, they would tire of the game. They would drop their gazes and one of them even had the temerity to snatch Pigafetta's paper from his hands and stuff it into his mouth before any of the men standing nearby could stop him. The crew merely laughed at Pigafetta's dismay. "Why bother teaching savages?" said one. "They are beyond redemption. They will never be able to enter the Kingdom of Heaven."

During the fourth week of their captivity, the guards relaxed their vigilance. One morning, the crew awoke and made the discovery that one of the giants was missing. The iron bolt that had held his shackles had been pulled clean out of the deck. Since the nearest island was several leagues away, it was understood that the giant must have drowned. All that day and the next, the sailors felt becalmed; each man became lost in his own private thoughts.

Each imagined a different fate for the giant: some said he had harnessed himself to the back of a giant sea turtle (since such creatures had been seen, miles from the nearest land) and had found his way home. Others said he had sunk like a stone to the bottom of the ocean since the chains that bound his ankles together would have hampered his ability to swim. Others maintained that the captive had a magical ability to assume the form of another creature and was, even now, circling the ship in the form of a leaping dolphin.

The remaining three captives chattered and gesticulated wildly, as though they had taken leave of their senses. Sometimes what they said sounded like "Oogh, oogh, oogh!" Other times, it sounded like "Bak, bak, bak!" Still other times it sounded like "Wa-see, wa-see, wa-see." Their hand movements, up and down in the air like the flapping wings of strange birds, seemed to bode ill. One by one, the crew of the Trinidad were felled by a strange sickness that left them giggling weakly, like silly children.

In the end, Magellan had no choice. He had entertained a fanciful ambition to present the captives to his patron, Carlos I, as a gift. Many times he had imagined the scene: the King, surrounded by all his courtiers. Magellan's entrance, announced by the chamberlain. Magellan imagined Carlos I leaning forward and looking closely at each captive with a familiar, penetrating gaze.

But now Magellan saw that it would not do. The natives' madness was infecting the entire ship.

He had never shrunk from making the hard decisions. When the conspiracy of Juan de Cartagena and the priest, Pero Sanchez de la Reina, had been exposed, he had ordered them put ashore on a tiny island, just off the coast of Brazil. He had left them no stores of food, no weapons, no means of protecting themselves from the harsh winter that was to come. The two had implored his forgiveness. They had fallen to their knees on the sand and wept. They had invoked his mother and the King, all the angels and saints in heaven. Magellan had ordered the ships to cast off. He had never looked back.

One night, the order was given to toss the three remaining captives overboard. Because of their iron fetters, they sank quickly. What the crew remembered most clearly was the complete and utter silence with which the captives entered the sea. Long after the giants had disappeared in the waves, the men of the Trinidad remained looking out at the dark water. They listened with an ache in their hearts to the sighing of the wind in the sails, the creaking of the rigging, and the wave-sounds of the great ocean, which had never seemed so feminine as it did that night. It seemed almost as if a heart was beating down there, miles below them.

None felt the loss of the captives more keenly than Pigafetta. Brooding in his cabin a few days after the captives had been thrown overboard, he wrote in his journal: "The sea is our mother. And, like a mother, she remembers everything and forgives all. *Dios vos salve, capitan-general.*"

A few months later, when Magellan lay dying in the surf off Cebu, he would remember the first giant. He would remember the way the man appeared, dancing and laughing on the beach. He would remember, as well, the expression in the eyes of the four captives, an expression he had interpreted to mean sadness, but which he now knew had been something else entirely.

Struck with the enormity of this insight, Magellan cried out, "For God—!" At the very last, his mind had been opened. His heart, bursting with gratitude at this knowledge, which he recognized instinctively as a gift, began a strange new rhythm in his chest.

The man who stood before him, his cutlass upraised, took no notice of Magellan's strange utterance and drove his blade home.

The beach he stood on, fringed with coconut trees, stretched widely in every direction. Behind the trees lay a profound and mysterious silence.

This island was somewhat larger than the others and had a backbone of rugged mountains. The weary sailors had cast anchor only a few days before. They had spent their time searching the interior for potable water but found none and had been forced to slake their thirst with the juice of fallen coconuts.

At daybreak one morning, the lookout spotted lazy tendrils of smoke rising from the lower slopes of the mountain. Magellan ordered the men to gather together coins, rosary beads, and a few other nearly worthless trinkets.

He and several men then pushed off in a long boat. The crew watched anxiously as they berthed on the sand and entered the immense silence of the forest. In each of the watching sailors' minds was the one question, only the one. The island was implacable and unmoved. Nothing stirred, not even a shadow, in the green density.

When the sun was almost at its zenith, the watch gave a shout. The men were returning. The sailors rushed to the deck and saw first one man, then another and another. Blood was streaming down their faces.

Only that morning, Lapu-Lapu had asked the *babaylan*, the oldest woman in the village, "What do you see?"

"Light the fires," she had replied. "Tonight you will eat well." Lapu-Lapu then began to sharpen his blade.

An hour later, he returned to the seeress. "Shall I kill today?" he asked. "What shall I kill?"

"You will find it on the beach" she had said. "It will have a powerful magic. Kill it there! Whatever happens, it must not be allowed to board the ship."

Lapu-Lapu thought of this now as he lunged. The white man staggered. The chief felt his blade slice through something soft and unresisting. His blood thirst rose. He drew his blade back halfway and then pushed forward once more. There was so much force in the second thrust that Lapu-Lapu found himself losing his balance.

There they knelt, the two enemies, chest to chest in an awkward embrace. The smell of the strange white man repulsed Lapu-Lapu. With a great yell, he leaped to his feet, pulling the blade back, slick with the other's blood. He lowered it to the surf and watched the water lapping over it. The blood spun away in trickles, in whorls. The white stranger fell heavily forward. Lapu-Lapu turned his back. Had the stranger been alive, he would have avenged this insult. But Lapu-Lapu sensed that he was dead.

The rest of the attackers crowded closely 'round. All that the horrified witnesses on the ships could see now was the furious thrusting of the natives' wooden spears. Darkness eddied in the water around their calves.

A few meters away, several of Lapu-Lapu's men had set on the remaining Castilians. In spite of their armor, their carapaces of metal which glinted so astonishingly in the sun, the strangers looked cowed and diminished. Two had managed to fight their way to the longboat. A man who appeared to be the pilot had even managed to get one leg over the side. But it was too late. Though the men on the ships shouted, desperately urging their companions on, not one of the landing party managed to escape.

Pigafetta witnessed all from the deck of the Trinidad. Heartbroken, he was nevertheless still bound by duty. Perhaps late that night or the next, we know he retrieved his journal from its leather case and gave a painstaking and excruciatingly detailed description of the tragedy. The last words of Pigafetta's journal, of which only one copy remains, were:

"That was how they slew our mirror, our light, our comfort, and our true guide. In the Year of Our Lord, April 1521."

– 0 –

EL REY, FELIPE II

Preceding His Majesty were a dozen servants wearing white caps and carrying gleaming astronomical instruments. Not long after, the jester mounted a marble bench and announced, "His Catholic Royal Majesty!" The court rose as one. Felipe II entered the hall.

The monarch moved forward, crossing a white tile floor on which pointed black stars twinkled. On either side of him were two perfectly straight lines of milk-white floor lamps. He wore a long, black velvet coat extending to his knees, its collar studded with emeralds. An emerald in the shape of a shooting star gleamed on the right side of his chest. More emeralds glowed in the King's gold crown.

Rustling of garments. The hum of voices like the droning of bees, transporting Legazpi to the orange groves of his youth. The light slanting from the high, stained-glass windows was the sun; it struck his father's orange groves, giving the fruit the burnished sheen of gold. Felipe II mounted the dais at the center of the hall.

Execrations against the crown, Magellan's death, the insult to Our Royal Person. Reports of several of his crew taken prisoner and turned into slaves.

Legazpi startled at that last. Turned into slaves? *Slaves?*

A delicate ivory rosary dangled from His Majesty Felipe II's right wrist. Around his neck was a ruff of golden fleece. A generous application of rose powder lent a trace of color to His Majesty's long, pale cheeks.

Then began the recitation:

De las Islas Filipinas. Heretico. Paganos. Esta tierra fué la primera. Incorporo a la Corona de España. La primera Misa. Higantes. Me parece que. Instrumento. Tordesillas.

Ah! This last. The Treaty of Tordesillas, in which Pope Alexander VI had drawn a line from pole to pole, dividing the world like the two halves of an orange: everything east of the line henceforth belonged to Portugal, everything west to Spain, thereby ending centuries of struggle between the two arch-rivals. The world seemed at last able to contain the two countries' teeming ambitions, ambitions that had taken root and flowered in a dream born as a whisper in the ear of a friend of a friend of a friend: Francisco Serrao, Portuguese, who wrote to the Crown from the Moluccas, in words both ardent and teasing. "Gold and riches," Serrao wrote. "Spices and women." The voyages that followed the signing of the treaty: Vasco Nuñez de Balboa; Garcia Jofre de Loaisa; Sebastian Cabot; Alvaro de Saavedra; Ruy Lopez de Villalobos.

The Loaisa expedition! Who in Spain had not heard of the disastrous outcome: It took the incompetent commander 10 months to get seven ships through the Straits of Magellan. By then, Loaisa was dead, one of his captains murdered, and twenty-five of his crew held for ransom by the Portuguese in Pernambuco.

The Cabot and Saavedra expeditions did not even make it as far as the Moluccas.

Villalobos's ships, larger and better rigged, was able to reach the Las Islas Filipinas, but Villalobos received a less than kindly reception and lost his nerve. He left the islands after barely two weeks.

Why, Legazpi wondered, did His Majesty insist on another expedition? His determination bordered on obsession.

After Magellan had been felled on that remote beach, the crew hastily re-fit the two remaining boats. Six weeks later, they departed the islands. Then followed what, in Legazpi's opinion, was the real story: The pilot Elcano plotted the return home across the Indian Ocean and up the Atlantic, a feat of seamanship that had yet to be equaled in the annals of navigation. It took a year of wandering and storms and battling strange sea creatures with red eyes and enormous maws and being saved, over and over again, by prayers to the Virgin and to Saint Judas, the patron saint of lost causes. They had skirmished with the Dutch and the Portuguese, fled English ships bearing down with massive cannon, and lost many of the crew to disease and simple cowardice. By the time the Victoria limped into harbor at Sanlucar de Barrameda, her crew were down to Elcano and just seventeen men. Eighteen skeletons.

Each of the 30 were interviewed with the utmost thoroughness. They scattered across Europe, to sign on to other voyages or, like Pigafetta, to write chronicles of their experiences.

That pilot, that Basque, Sebastian Elcano, who had brought survivors of Magellan's expedition home—he signed on with Loaisa, who was an incompetent. Elcano died on the Pacific, scarcely halfway to the islands.

Our cousin Portugal refuses our claim to Africa and makes discovery of lands to the East, including the Filipinas. But Spain asserts, by the Grace of God, its Kingly right.

A fretful look appeared on the face of His Royal Majesty.

His Majesty's natural speaking voice was high, almost girlish. Now, it seemed to stutter, an impediment apparently in his throat. Legazpi watched His Catholic Majesty pause, swallow. Eventually, His Majesty resumed, seeming to round out each syllable unnecessarily.

Oro. Carried by the mountain rivers. Down to the plains of Luzon.

Legazpi thought: The pay? No, do not even bring up the idea of coin.

You will be compensated.

The unspoken contract: *Whatever is not provided can be taken.*

With such stories, who would not sign on? Legazpi would be turning crew away.

The Royal Dwarves, standing on either side of the Sovereign, clapped. The courtiers, Legazpi included, bowed their heads.

His Royal Majesty gestured to a page. The page approached, bearing before him on stiffly extended arms a large globe, almost as large as his head. He had practiced this task; his steps never faltered. He arrived at His Majesty's feet, bowed, and raised the globe over his head for the monarch's perusal. His Majesty extended a slender finger. Tap, tap, tap. A scent of cloves wafted from his sleeve. The boy remained in that position despite the trembling of his arms.

At length, His Majesty waved an arm at the boy, You may go. The boy retreated while remaining bent at the waist, taking the globe with him.

His Majesty returned his gaze to Legazpi.

The monarch looked him over—up, down, up, down. A look of blank confusion came over his features. Legazpi was elderly, past 50, there was no disguising his years. His face was weathered and marked with smallpox scars.

He had spent decades commandeering. The sea takes its toll.

Yet, he had come with effusive endorsements, from everyone ranging from the *Gubernador General* of Nueva España to the illustrious members of the Council of the Indies.

Felipe II glanced at his ministers. They nodded solemnly.

Arise. Legazpi rose. *Approach and kneel.* Legazpi knelt.

His Royal Majesty lowered his scepter and tapped first Legazpi's right shoulder, then his left. The taps on Legazpi's shoulder felt more like blows.

He has done this many times. My shoulders will have a bruise.

Legazpi's headache, which began several days ago, now bloomed inside his head, a poisonous flower.

"Is there anything you wish to say?" The Monarch said.

What could be said? "Your Serene Highness, allow me to express my deepest gratitude for your gracious liberality," Legazpi responded.

There was movement, followed by a low ripple of laughter. Legazpi lifted his head and saw the Royal Dwarves mimicking the King's gestures exactly.

His Royal Majesty declared he would grant Legazpi five ships. Two ships more than El Viejo expected. Each would be fitted with the usual complement of bronze cannon. And 500 men, he added, almost as an afterthought.

Legazpi thought about how those ships would sit in the water, attracting privateers the way honey does flies. He imagined Portuguese and Dutch and English sails bearing down swiftly in fresh wind.

Five always a magical number to Legazpi.

The fifth of March, his wedding to Doña Isabela de Garce. The five most beautiful lines in El Cid. The five journeys he had made.

Legazpi had five children: his firstborn, Elena, died when she was five. Friday, the fifth day of the week.

The woman he left behind in Nueva España, who was not his wife—he had left her after five years, when she was five months heavy with child. He has received letters from her, telling him about their child. Almost grown, now.

One, two. And three and four and five landings on an empty beach. One and three, four and five squares of light on the floor of the *Royal Audiencia*. The journey, it was estimated, would take five years. He would be an old man, then, when he returned. *If* he returned.

His Royal Majesty intoned, *May we remind you of Our Majesty's determination. May we remind you of the consequences of rebellion against Our Most Holy Selves.*

Legazpi placed his hand over his heart, bowed his head and said, "Allow me, the least of your servants, to kiss your Royal feet and hands."

He heard a voice behind him: "Rise." Legazpi's headache shrieked. Someone behind him whispered, directly into the shell of his left ear, "The bones are of the utmost importance. Magellan's bones. *Reliquarios.* His Majesty must have them."

Legazpi nodded and thought: I shall return with *someone's* bones. The King will not be displeased.

The white sails. The green oceans.
Everywhere a Spanish ship went, that was Spain. The ship's deck became Mother. The ports they entered were also Mother. The Mother's embrace spanned worlds.

"Return them to Ourselves, and you shall be richly rewarded."

"May I assure Your Majesty that I, Ever Thine Loyal Servant, shall, with sword in hand, perform my duties, even to the death."

The Augustinian friar, Andres de Urdaneta, was to be his pilot. An Augustinian? Legazpi had never heard of this man. Nevertheless, if His Royal Majesty had chosen him, he was undoubtedly the best.

Felipe II then gave Legazpi a tight smile, waved a pale white hand, and exited the throne room.

Courtiers sniggered behind their palms. No one knew why Lopez de Legazpi, a 51-year-old from Zumarraga, was given command. No one expected him to succeed when others, much younger and much more capable, had failed. *It is all for show.*

What does it matter, Miguel Lopez de Legazpi thought. *Let His Majesty have his games. I shall be all solicitude and fervor.*

Legazpi's wife, Doña Isabela. Her hair, her thick dark braid. Not diminished in the least by the years.

Pray for thine husband, Doña Isabela. It may be five years, it may be ten. It may be fifteen years. It may be never. Pray for thine husband.

Crafty, Legazpi was. He learned his sea-lore young, leaving his ancestral home at twelve, hanging about the port in Cadiz. He knew how to get his men through.

He pored over Magellan's ships' logs and the statements of various witnesses, not raising his head until the candles in his room were about to go out.

These words of Pigafetta, written some 50 odd years before:

If only the pilot had not found the current that led us to the shining archipelago. The date, the 31st of March, in the Year of Our Lord Fifteen-hundred and Twenty-one. If only, if only, if only. His lieutenant beside him in the surf, killed too. What a reward for his loyalty!

That was how they slew our mirror, our light, our comfort, and our true guide. In the Year of Our Lord, April 1521.

Three ships, balanced on the surface of the world, totally alone. Legazpi tried to imagine it.

Legazpi launched from Acapulco, on the Atlantic Coast of Nueva España. His heart, which had been a clenched fist since he first received his task, eased. It had been years, but he remembered well a time in his life when he was young and exuberant. Now that old curiosity about the world was returning, confidence building with each passing swell.

The ships sailed south, tracing the coast of Brazil. There were furious storms. Scurvy decimated the crew. Shipworm attacked the hulls. They veered west, toward Guam and the Ladrones, which astrologers said was only a few days sailing. Legazpi felt the ache for land even more heatedly. He drove his men, so great was his need.

They crossed the Equator. It took them 56 days, half the time it had taken Magellan.

A member of the crew swore he saw a flock of blackbirds. What were these emblems? Harbingers of doom? Dark magic? *They are coming, they are coming*, he wailed.

Conjurations, Legazpi scoffed.

Another man swore he saw a wild-eyed owl. The man's eyes rolled into the back of his head. Juan de Salcedo seized the man and clouted him into silence.

Too much, these prophecies of destruction. Legazpi was young once. But look, now, where he was. Gone, gone, gone.

They anchored in Guam, whose inhabitants robbed them, treacherously murdering one of their crew. They saw one island, and another, and yet more. Legazpi ordered his pilots to continue steering west.

They began to see boats: needle-like things, carved out of tree trunks and wide enough just for one man to sit. They moved swiftly, trembling shadows over the ocean swells.

After two days meandering, a man swore he saw the Blessed Virgin walking toward the ships at dawn. But there was a mist over the water, so he could not be sure whether her feet were atop the waves. And then they spotted the first Giant approaching. The chieftain Sikatuna.

The chieftain's arms were covered in blue and red ink: cresting waves, fantastical foliage. Sikatuna's hair was long and oiled and smelled of rot. Sikatuna gestured to his warriors. Who, he announced, would be strong enough to pass beyond? No one.

Warm welcomes. Smiles.

The crew cowered. Legazpi extended his hand. Sikatuna stood with one hip jutting out. *Like a woman,* Legazpi thought.

A nerve twitched in Legazpi's right cheek.

Sikatuna's gaze drifted to the right, to Juan de Salcedo. Juan de Salcedo, who turned 17 a day after the ships crossed the Equator. The boy's eyes were the flat grey of stone. *Do not look at him,* Legazpi growled. *It is I you must deal with.*

Sikatuna could barely countenance the odor of Legazpi and his men, it is a loathsome odor, more akin to that of animals.

They travel without women and children. Their God is a flayed man nailed to a cross. If this is how they treat their God, how will they treat his people? They want everything: the water, the land, the sky. To own, this is all they want.

I shall leave them nothing, Sikatuna thought. *Nothing, nothing, nothing. Despite their flashing mirrors, their spears that spit fire and rake the ground with holes.*

To his people, Sikatuna said: *We will vanish them with our powerful magic. The way we vanished the Other Gold Seeker. Maayo gid, he died on the sand. Here we have kept him, all these years. There he is, there he is. His sun-bleached bones. What will they promise in exchange?*

The *babaylan* sang:

Good news.
If they seek fresh water to drink, the water will curl back, leaving them stones.

If they take our trees, the trees will turn into fierce lizards.
If they seek our homes, they will find not one dwelling.
They will be struck with uneasiness, unable to rest but unable to find.

The sailors heard the *babaylan's* voice, wafting across the water, the strange ululations of her speech.

Get up, children.
Your mother has gone home.
She lives now.
She has awakened.

The sun reached the highest point. The yellow orb clicked into place, like a pebble finding a groove. The ocean breathed waves of heat. Someone on the beach keened her distress. The giants surged yelling from the line of trees toward the black ships. Legazpi's cannons were ready for them. A few of the giants fell, but most were still on their feet, heading into the surf, into the first wave.

We are brothers.
We are kin.
We are strong.
Together with Skydwelling gods,
We will vanish the Enemy.

At day's end, there was no clear victor. Sikatuna signaled for truce. Two days later, he and six of his warriors clambered aboard the *extranjero's* boat.

Unlike Magellan, Legazpi was not interested in taking them captive. Instead, he reached into his boot and produced a short knife. He cut his forearm deeply, then held it up, letting the blood drip into a small bowl.

Sikatuna looked at the blood as if mesmerized. It was the same color as his own, who knew!

Legazpi gestured to Sikatuna that he should follow suit. He handed the bowl to Sikatuna. Sikatuna accepted it. He brought the bowl to his nose and took a long, deep breath.

A murmur rose from the gathered Spaniards. *What is he—? At* length, when he had smelled to his satisfaction, he handed back the bowl and held up his forearm. Then, with his own dagger, Sikatuna made the cut. A quick slice, and then Sikatuna held his arm over the bowl, letting his blood drip into the bowl and mingle with that of the stranger.

Sikatuna's blood. The stranger's blood. A spell. And all the wars he had fought, and all the children he had fathered, what were they for?

The boy came forward and brandished a dagger in Sikatuna's face.

The boy's skin was flushed with heat, his hair longer than the others, curly and oiled, like a woman's, his eyes cold, cold as a lizard's. And his smell! His smell struck absolute terror in Sikatuna's heart.

The boy pointed at Sikatuna's chest with his blade; Sikatuna had an image of his own blood mingling with the sea surf. Sikatuna shut his eyes. He felt himself become black night water.

To buy his people time, Sikatuna decided to pretend. *I am lowly, I am humble, I submit.* Sikatuna did not know that it was hopeless, that time was the one thing he and his people did not have.

The next morning, the black ships began moving away.

There were other islands. Sebu, ruled by the woman Agowa, also known as the Half Queen. Her husband, a great warrior, had been felled by a sickness. Now, Agowa had two sons to raise, and a people to lead, and she was weary of doing battle with other tribes. Wishing to avoid outright confrontation, she welcomed the strangers with practiced smiles.

"What is the purpose of your journey," she asked. The boy with the cold eyes spun lie after lie. The Half Queen was dazed by the enigma of his presence.

Soon, everyone on the islands would know the boy, Juan de Salcedo, grandson of Miguel de Legazpi, Lizard, Snake, Vanquisher. Chiefs would crouch under his conquering sword. Everywhere he went, he reminded people about Magellan's bones.

A seeress tried to warn Agowa: this boy possessed an all-conquering thirst to subdue. Agowa learned too late: what the boy loved most of all was islands.

Most Powerful Sire, the man kneeling before Felipe II began, *Your Most Humble and Loyal Servant, El Adelantado Miguel Lopez de Legazpi, has made landfall in the great Archipelago, with three of his five ships. They are now on the island of Panay, where they begin construction of a fort at the harbor of Oton and send word that they await Your Majesty's instruction.*

His Royal Majesty turned his face to the court. There was weariness in it. The courtiers were puzzled. They were here to celebrate a successful expedition, were they not? They itched to know the contents of a recent missive sent by the Pope to Felipe II.

Rustling of silks, as the court gave the ceremonial welcome.

The papal envoy, a man with a long black beard, came forward and knelt.

$$- 0 -$$

WHO OWNS THIS ISLAND?

Bukay and two of his sons were on the beach, the day the strangers arrived. They were surprised to see the boat where no boat had ever been, not since as far back as Bukay could remember. It was a *parao*, not as large as the *vintas* of the Moro pirates. And it was resting on what they considered their beach, in the island's southernmost point, a rocky shore riddled with limestone caves. Hinoba-an was their name for it.

The boat lay at rest on a narrow strip of black sand. Translucent sea crabs scuttled around, waving their pincers in panic.

The first to disembark were soldiers. Ka Bukay counted three. Two were lifting a large burlap sack of rice. The soldiers were followed by a man in the clothing of a priest, young from the agile way he leaped onto the sand.

Bukay motioned to his sons to hide.

The soldiers spotted Bukay, standing uncertainly at the edge of the forest. He had taken the wise precaution of laying down his bow and arrows.

"You there!" one of the soldiers called out to Bukay. "Who owns this island?"

Bukay knew Spanish, for he was intelligent and had worked for a time in a mission on the next island.

"God. *Dios*," Bukay answered.

"No," the soldier responded. "Spain owns this island." An answer which amazed Bukay, because he had never met anyone who put Spain on a higher footing than God.

The soldier then removed a sword from his belt and pushed it deep into the sand. Bukay watched as the young man—the priest—raised his hands to the heavens and made supplication, insistent and odd-sounding.

"Father, what are they doing?" Bukay's older son, Labaw, asked. The boy had restless eyes, which followed every gesture the way waves wash onto a beach.

"Making an offering to their god," Bukay said.

They watched from the cover of the trees as the white men knelt, heads uncovered, and the young priest said words not Spanish but not native either, and made a sign over each kneeling man's head.

Later that night, Bukay returned to his hut at the edge of a clearing where he lived with his wife and their three children. When he told his wife, she grew pale. "What do you think they will do?" she asked.

Bukay sighed. "Whatever they like. They are Spaniards."

- 0 -

TOAD

I'm a spotter. I'm good at spotting people, what their weaknesses are.

I look for what feels familiar, it's that simple. It's that easy.
I see you, gentle men and women. I see you.
You may smile, smile, smile. Always smile, smile, smile.
But all the time I'm waiting. Waiting for you to slip.
I'm thinking about power. Always thinking about power.

The First Mark

"Come with us, we'll show you," I say to the short man.
"I don't trust you, I don't know you," he says, pulling slightly away from me. "Why should I go with you?"
"Sounds like a Wookie," I say to Joe.
"Sometimes," I say to the short man, going right up to him, "sometimes you just have to get out."

Victims aren't always helpless. Does that sound like an oxymoron?

Is it strange, that I'm asking?
The world is made up of those who control and those who are controlled *by*. That's just the way it is. No use, as they say, wishing for the moon.
Perhaps you think I sound manipulative? Cold?
All I'm saying is: Don't get a wife. Don't, don't, don't.
Or you bury yourself. In a tomb bigger than Arundel's.

The Second Mark

As to how the situation with Molly developed.

She was a toad. She had big, gelatinous eyes. Why was she squatting in my life, what cause did I give her ever? Tears always spilling from her eyes, towards what end?

She called me a brute. Oh la-di-day, oh la-di-day.

"Molly," I said, "Is there someone you love? More than yourself, I mean? Because six days a week I toil. Driving that cab around."

"You make me sick, Molly," I said. "The way you're always making things all out of proportion. And are you a pauper? Do we live like paupers?"

Molly crying and rubbing her eyes. She going: "Why do Dorothy and the others get to live like queens? Up-lane, in the big houses that always smell sweet, like roses? And we ourselves smell like tinned meat."

"You seemed to like it once, Molly," I said. "Ten years ago, you'd have no complaints. You seemed to like it, remember? I would tickle your bare feet—Good God! Unspeakable! I must have been mad. And if I were brave enough—Stuff your cooking and your cleaning! And the three wee nippers, good Lord! The way the lot of you eat—! Has you starved? Has any of you? What dreams I had once, Molly. That's the stuff."

You're a toad, Molly, Molly, Molly. And again, I said Molly, Molly, Molly. You go hop hop hop, hop hop hop, giving me the stink-eye. Hunkers hard like a cow's, but no milk in your udders. Lips cold as snow.

Now, only the Lord knows. Only the Lord knows why.

Being a victim is like having a smell. When some people drink a lot, their skin begins to smell like corned beef. It has nothing to do with cleanliness. The smell comes from somewhere deep inside.

And this particular smell, the smell of a victim, is a lure.

But oh, that's all water under the bridge now.

I'm as jointed armor now, true as a knight's steel.

Bees sting and ducks swim. Sniffing out marks—that's what I'm good at. That's what I do.

– 0 –

SAND

After I had stolen my mother's Chopard diamond earrings, the ones my father had given her for their 20th wedding anniversary, I didn't know what to do with myself. I ended up far from home, on an island clear across the ocean. I found a thatched hut on a narrow beach. Every morning, I listened to fishermen pull their boats up on the shore. People would appear and haggle over fish with snub heads and flat fish shaped like half-moons and long, silvery fish that looked like sardines, only ten times bigger.

I was going to do something, but I didn't know what. I felt brave, I felt I would never fail as long as I had the earrings with me. I sewed them into a little pouch on the inside of the waistband of my jeans, and I wore just the one pair of jeans, day in and day out. They were soft and loose, ripped at the knees. I didn't have to pretend: I was what I was. I was crazy. I was living.

I met a fisherman named Ben Hur. He told me he had a cross-eyed wife and a son born with a harelip. At night, Ben Hur would show up dangling two bottles of San Miguel. I couldn't stop looking at the corded muscles of his arms, the thin leather straps that he wore around both wrists.

The first time he showed up, it made me nervous. But he told me he'd asked permission from his wife, who said to him one day, "There's an American woman living by herself on the beach. Go see if she needs anything."

I felt I'd come to the right place. I felt I'd found home. No more wondering what to have for breakfast—yogurt or cereal, or both? No more deciding between green salad or gummy bears or between root beer or tequila. No more wondering whether or not

I could go for a month or two months without having a job. No more decisions, big or small, of any kind. Being an American was so exhausting.

The only question now was: what did Ben Hur want? Or, rather, what *would* he want? And when I found out, would I measure up? Would I be the answer?

Dearest Dad owned a successful jewelry business—how do you think my mother ended up with so many earrings? I tried to convince him to give me a loan to cover my rent. But he was still mad at me from the time I'd charged $20,000 to his credit card during my semester abroad in Salamanca. Dearest Dad had a long memory. Cross him once, and he never forgot. Never. He had the memory of an elephant and the sensitivity of a teenager—a bad combination. I hated him, but I needed him, too.

Once, I imagined that stealing my mother's Chopard earrings would change my life in a good way. After all, my mother had a lot of them. Tiffany and Cartier. Van Cleef & Arpels. My father spoiled her to a degree that caused talk in our hometown, a place where rich women went shopping in Bangkok or Mumbai, London or Paris.

At one time, my mother acquired a fascination with matryoshka dolls. Every month for five years, my father gave her a new matryoshka doll. They weren't the fake kind of matryoshka dolls you found in gift shops. They were real Russian matryoshka dolls, handcrafted in St. Petersburg when the city was still called St. Petersburg. Which meant they were old. Antique. There were so many dolls, they filled every room in the house. After my mom lost interest in them, the way she always lost interest in everything, the dolls had to be given away to a local museum.

And then my dreams started. I dreamt of matryoshka dolls, dancing around my bed. I dreamt my boyfriend, Melvin, had turned into a matryoshka doll. He stood next to me, making matryoshka doll faces. His severely penciled brows seemed to acquire the intensity of lightning bolts. "Fuck!" I said. "Melvin, stop making matryoshka doll faces at me." Melvin disappeared, and in his place was a dancing chicken. A dancing grilled chicken. A barbecue stick protruding through each wing. I couldn't believe Melvin had turned into a chicken and that I was now required to eat him. Then I woke up. Then I knew that if I didn't steal my mother's Chopard earrings and soon, I'd always be the kind of person whose boyfriend turned into a matryoshka doll that made faces at her.

When the Chopard earrings were in my hand—or, rather, when they were in my purse, or—what am I talking about? I never owned a purse, only a little silk pouch my grandmother had given me when I was 12 and which was now significantly frayed and threadbare, which was dangerous for the contents, particularly for Chopard earrings—anyway, *when I had the earrings with me*, I felt light. I felt I was floating through the air, and down the stairs, even though I wasn't actually taking another step. It was like the way people moved in *True Blood*. Fast, and then still. Fast, and then still. Like my body was being moved by an invisible conveyor belt. One which kept stuttering.

I got on a plane, still in a fog. It seemed days before I looked out the plane window and saw anything other than white. The plane swooped low over green fields and rivers. The landing was hard, and I lurched forward in my seat. But the minute I felt the blast of hot air outside on the tarmac, I felt, for the first time since I'd done that crazy thing, whole.

There is something about the sound of church bells that reminds me of my childhood. It's a sad sound because, of course, it's been a while since I was a child. When I was 21, I moved to New York, entered grad school, and met Melvin. He was tall and blonde and had soft grey eyes. We spent a blissful summer backpacking across Europe. I did most of the carrying; Melvin claimed he had a bad back, but I'd seen him lift heavy things like encyclopedias when he thought I wasn't paying attention.

He proposed in Perugia. We were married over there and for two months—in July and almost all of August—it was unbelievably exciting. I almost believed our lives would always be a series of long, blissful, romantic adventures.

Two years later, I'd moved back home, Melvin had metamorphosed into a matryoshka doll, and the only way I could see to break out of the rut was to steal my mother's Chopard earrings.

One day, I felt two hot tears crawling down my cheeks. It must have been a Sunday; in fact, I'm almost sure it was. From far away, beyond the line of coconut trees that lined the beach, church bells were ringing. I decided it was pathetic to build my days around waiting for Benhur to show up with his two bottles of Ginebra. Then and there, I decided to make a little excursion to the public market.

I had been living on nothing but the flesh of raw coconuts. My neck and arms felt gaunt. I didn't have a mirror, but I was pretty sure I looked awful. I was weak and wanted to taste something different—taro root, carrot, or something healthy. To eat too much of anything, even something as exotic as coconut meat, eventually makes one unhappy. So, I thought the first step to feeling better was to vary my diet.

And in the market were all the most marvelous things. First of all, the smell was not that bad. The market was a row of stalls, around which shallow trenches had been dug. People threw fish scales and fish tails into the trenches, and then at night stray animals came along and helped themselves to these delights.

I realized that morning in the market that people were not giving way to allow me to get closer to the tables where the produce was displayed. In fact, in their jostling was a kind of rudeness that shocked and then scared me. All along I had thought that these little people found me amusing: a weird American woman who liked to tell unintelligible stories and drink beer with the fishermen on the beach. I thought they were developing affection for me. I tried so hard to learn their language and didn't care if people laughed. I was not above letting Benhur cop a feel. Of course, my breasts were not the melon-like appendages of actresses like Scarlett Johansson or Jennifer Lawrence. I had always been a little flat-chested and now that my diet was so limited, my breasts were terrible to look at.

I found myself crying and saying, "Please, please," and finally someone threw a tiny fish at me. It hit me in the face and stung quite a bit, but I caught it in one hand and was able to gasp, *"Pila ini?"* which I think means "How much?" And the fish woman spat and said something like *Scram*. Of course, not that word exactly, because she was speaking her native tongue, but I understood what she meant immediately.

And so I took the little fish home and when Benhur came that night he offered to cook it for me, and he coaxed a small fire out of some coconut palm fronds, and then he had about ¾ of the fish and I was still hungry, but I couldn't speak because he wanted me to do something with my mouth, and, because of his kindness, I could not refuse him.

Before this, I had tried so hard, in all my conversations with Benhur, to keep asking questions about his family. I knew his wife's name was Silveth. I knew his son was named Jesus Lord. I thought that invoking his family constantly would be a kind of protection. Afterwards, I realized Benhur was not fooled. He knew I was alone, completely alone, in the whole wide world, and that no one would come to my aid.

Melvin had forced me to ask my parents for the $30,000. I told my parents he needed the money to set up a chain of sandwich eateries in Malaysia. The chain would be called Big Boy. As I was describing Melvin's plans to my parents, their eyes got big and round and they even ended up asking if Melvin was sure he only needed $30,000. Later I found that instead of using the money for his start-up, he went to Las Vegas (he told me he was attending a restaurant convention) and spent all the money playing blackjack and poker. His luck was bad, that's why he felt he had to keep playing—because he believed in the eternal cycle of inevitability: in other words, he truly believed one could not keep losing at blackjack forever.

When he came home, he cried and confessed and I truly felt sorry for him. I was an unsupportive, suspicious wife—a dominatrix, no less—and I had reduced my husband to blubbering in front of me like a baby. Which, as any therapist will tell you, is the fastest way to erode a marriage.

After a year of living on canned beans and eggs, I finally confessed to my parents what had happened to the money. Or, rather, I didn't confess. The taking of my mother's Chopard earrings was the closest I could come to admitting that I was a loser and a thief and would really amount to nothing. By this time, I knew for a fact that Melvin had done me wrong and I was not about to give him any of the money I stole from my parents. The earrings were mine, all mine! They would help me re-build my life, as soon as I was ready. In the meantime, I was too exhausted to do anything more than languish on a beach and try to disappear.

"The rains are coming," Benhur said one day. His English had improved markedly since his nighttime assignations with me. This should have made me proud, but it didn't. Instead, I listened dully and tried to work out what that would mean for me personally, to have the rains come.

"Pow!" Benhur said suddenly, pounding his fist into the sand. "Pow! Pow! Pow!"

It seemed as though he was trying to show me how hard the rain would fall.

"Moon," Benhur said. He made an O with his arms, clasping his palms around the hollow of air. "Current."

"What, Benhur?" I said. "What?"

"Boat!" Benhur said. He was practically screaming. "Boat! Boat! Boat!"

"You'll make a—a boat?" I said weakly. "Sail? A boat with sails?"

"No!" Benhur shouted. "No and no!"

Then I knew what he was saying. He was saying I should get on a boat and sail away. I should point the boat's prow to the far horizon. I should row unceasingly.

Perhaps I would fall out. Perhaps a storm would wash over the boat and hurl me into the ocean. Perhaps I would die of hunger or loneliness or both. Perhaps sharks would rip my boat and then my body to shreds.

But even if none of these things happened, I should never come back. Never, ever come back. He made it clear: he would not be responsible for me. It would be my failure, mine alone.

– 0 –

BODIES

The woman's body rested on the steps of the fountain in the middle of the plaza. It was Good Friday. The cathedral's bells rang out: Oh woe, woe! Condemnation from the pulpit.

Her husband, Adriano, had returned unexpectedly from a pilgrimage to Compostela and discovered her with her lover. Since she had given birth but two months before, she used fatigue as the reason for not accompanying her husband on his pilgrimage, and he believed her. The infant's cradle, Adriano saw, had been dragged close to the bed, the very bed where wrinkled sheets now gave off the musky scent of a lover's seed!

He began to beat them both. The lover was able to escape, but the beating of the woman continued for some time. Her calls for help were heard all over the neighborhood but no one came to her aid.

After an hour, there followed a long, mysterious silence that caused the neighbors to stay up all night, listening.

Then, a dragging sound. Sometimes interrupted by bouts of weeping.

At dawn the next day, as the market vendors were beginning to set up their tables, they saw the woman, sitting half-clothed on the steps of the fountain. The women crossed themselves.

There was a scarlet mouth on her white throat, a scarlet mouth that wept great gouts of dark blood. The spiteful sneered at her exposed breasts, still full of milk for the infant she bore just two months earlier. Eventually, a few brave men approached the broken woman and draped a blanket over her.

In the meantime, her husband had fled, leaving behind his three children, who were taken in by the woman's family.

Her brothers searched for Adriano. For, adulteress though their sister may have been, the family had wished for a different way for her to expiate her sin. They declared she would willingly have taken the habit, if such an offer had been made.

Where was Adriano now? No one knew whether he escaped or whether he chose to end his life by jumping into the Segura. If the latter, then his body would eventually surface. Unless the current had pulled it out to sea.

Bodies circle. There was a strange magnetic pull under the river, determining the direction of the currents. But, in the case of the murdered woman, whose body was left to wander the square, the mystery was never solved.

Her brothers eventually grew sick of the sight of her and tried to bury her in that section of the cemetery reserved for the indigent: no headstone was erected over her grave, no one visited, it was as if the murdered woman never existed, never married, never had children, never suffered, never had a lover.

But the next week she was there again on the steps of the fountain.

– 0 –

BRIDGING

A few weeks after Tom's funeral, the lawyer, Mr. Singer, read aloud the part of Tom's will that gave instructions on how to dispose of his remains: "I request that my body or any part may be used for the purpose of medical education or research. What is left of me shall be cremated and scattered in the bay."

Mr. Singer paused and looked at her, but Letty remained silent. Clearly, though, the lawyer had been expecting a response, and now he looked upon her silence as a form of resistance. "It is in the will," Mr. Singer said. "If it is in the will, you absolutely have to do it."

Letty nodded. There were so many things she hadn't known before Tom died: such as, how much money he really had. And whether he would be generous with her. When all was said and done, Letty paid very little attention. Instead, she stared in curiosity at Mr. Singer's navy-blue bow tie and the coppery sheen of his thinning hair.

The house was quiet—a good quiet, peaceful. She left her purse on the kitchen counter. It pleased her to think she did not have to worry about hiding things now. Tom had developed the habit of looking in her things, trying to "catch" her at something. She shook her head. Too much.

She brought in the papers. Almost every day, the *San Mateo County Times* published Letters to the Editor complaining of gangs and graffiti.

"In our own neighborhood!" a man complained. "I decided to walk around after dinner, last Monday. It was around nine o'clock at night. I was at the corner of Jefferson and Middlefield, waiting for the light to change, when two teen-agers came running out of nowhere. They knocked me down and stole my watch, my cell phone, and my wallet. I had $60 in cash. They hit my face so hard, I needed 14 stitches. The police have been asking for witnesses. No one wants to come forward."

The man was probably close to her age, Letty thought. She was 51.

Jefferson and Middlefield was right in front of the public library. Letty used to go almost every week, to check out books. Now she shuddered, upset for the man who had met with such violence. It was shocking.

Why did her son never call? He never, ever called, and she was so lonely.

He had more than enough money, that was why. When he was needy, back in the days when he was just starting grad school, he called often. Tom would be bad-tempered for days afterward.

That night, she dreamed about her husband. Tom said, "Letty, what are you doing? What are you doing?"

"Nothing," she said. "Just filling the time."

The Dream Tom snorted. She knew he didn't believe her.

It was a terrible dream. The worst she'd had in months. She took two Ambien, which was her almost-nightly intake now. She wondered how she'd explain that to her doctor. She thought again about her son, and about Tom's funeral, and about how hard it would be to keep up the garden, all by herself.

The bills came, she filled them out blankly, without checking her accounts. Truly, she knew she had more money than she really needed.

Tom's roses were dying. They'd been so pretty. He had tended them carefully. But after he died, she spent less and less time in the garden. She could tell, from the way the stems were gradually blackening, from the buds that never fully opened, that they were sick, starved for something.

Winter was settling in. Soon, the rains would come. But next year . . .?

"A job's a job, Tom," she found herself saying, aloud into the empty bedroom. "Like the 27 years I spent being married to you. And it didn't even do me any good. Ha ha ha!"

Her dream husband's face went sour. She remembered that look. He'd only been dead a few months, but she'd completely forgotten. After the dream, she remembered the look again.

Oh, oh, oh, oh, she went, and clutched her head. An ache began to spread from the base of her skull, outwards. It was spreading like a net. It had captured the nerves on her face. She was terrified of getting Bell's Palsy, which the women in her family had gotten, one by one, after they turned 40 or so. Not a single woman in her family had been spared.

Her mother's case had been the worst. Afterwards, her mother became fearful and inward-looking. Her aunts complained that Letty's mother had stopped accepting lunch or dinner invitations. On the occasions when she left her house, she wore large sunglasses that covered half her face and refused to take them off, even while eating, even though everyone could see, whenever she bent over a menu, that there was something wrong with the right cheek. That glimpse was enough. That was all she would offer anyone, that glimpse.

The morning after her bad dream, Letty realized that she might forget Tom's face, but never his smell. It clung to the pillowcases, even after she'd washed them several times. It had even, she thought, seeped into the mattress. She stripped the bed and began sleeping on the day bed in the guest room. The bedroom was too big, anyway. What she needed was safety, and the guest room, with its smaller dimensions, its hardly-used day bed and lone armchair, felt as if it could provide that.

Letty limped to the bathroom and turned on the light. Again, she was struck by how different the face in the mirror was from her own. She scarcely recognized that old woman with the wrinkles, the pouches, the deep furrows on either side of her mouth. That woman looked like an utter wreck.

She switched off the light, went back to bed, and pulled the comforter up to her chin. Then she stared at the ceiling for what seemed like hours. Finally, when she saw light slipping beneath the window curtains, she decided to get up and make herself a cup of tea.

Time passed slowly. She thought it was time for dinner, but then she'd glance at the clock in the kitchen and find out it was just 5 p.m. She tried not looking at her watch. She tried reading the papers or watching TV. The next time she glanced down at her watch, it was 5:26, and then later, 5:56.

She tried to punish herself by saying, "OK, no dinner until 8." Or she'd say: "No TV if you look at your watch more than three times in one afternoon."

But she got involved with watching "American Idol." There was a judge who reminded her of someone she'd known back in high school in the Philippines. Tom wasn't there to tease and say how silly the show was. She began watching every week, without fail.

She had met Tom in Cebu. She remembered just having gotten on a jeepney. Then a huge American man got in, taking up almost half the space. Everyone stared. Tom stared, too, but only at her. She'd felt a sudden heat creeping over her face and looked away. When she got off at her stop, he put out an arm, as if wanting to be courtly. But his forearm brushed her breasts. She shrank from him, and then he followed her.

They were married three months later, and the following year she was in America.

During her second year in America, she became pregnant. No need for her to take a test: she knew. She had three older sisters, each of whom had gotten pregnant when they were in their late teens. She knew the signs. Unlike her sisters, she had a husband. She felt proud.

When she told Tom, his face became a new face, darkened with anger.

"I will send you home!" he shouted. "I didn't bring you here to have babies!"

The current President was a man named Bush. She forgot this sometimes. It seemed there were so many people with that name, now.

The two mighty towers in New York were just a hole in the ground. She didn't understand Ground Zero, had to read articles over and over before it sank in what the reporters were writing about. One day she thought of taking a bus there, just to see. She was fascinated by the thought of the hole in the ground, and how 19 trailers were needed to sift through the dust, hunting the tiniest scrap of DNA. She thought of Tom, and wondered whether that was really him in the porcelain jar she had paid $129 for. Sometimes, she lifted the lid and looked at the gray ash inside. The first time, she had been surprised to discover something sparkly mixed in with the ash. After several weeks, she worked up the courage to dip a finger in the glittery ash. She placed the finger against her tongue. The thought of swallowing Tom was not pleasing. She trembled and spat and later avoided that spot on the carpet. Whenever she happened to catch a glimpse of the spot, she always thought the same thing: I must bring out the Resolve. But now it was months later, and the spot was still there. In fact, it was growing darker. Tom would have been incensed, if he could have seen it.

The one thing useful she had picked up from watching her husband was how to work the computer. It was a shiny gray square, which he kept tucked away in a drawer, and the few nights a week he was on it, he would cup his chin in his hand and chuckle. He kept the screen tilted away from the door, as if anticipating that she would stand there and look at him. When she would ask him what he was laughing about he always said, "None of your business."

"Take my hand, Div, take my hand!" Tom shouted.

They were on the beach in Guimaras. The waves were large at that time of year. No tourists about, but no help either, when a huge wave knocked them both out of the small motorboat Tom had rented for the day.

Water filled her nose and throat, it was awful. She didn't even know what she was doing, but she seemed to be sinking deeper and deeper into the ocean. Something slimy grabbed at her arms and she wanted to scream but her mouth wouldn't open. She thought of manta rays and eels.

Tom's voice came to her, thick and muffled. She gave one last mighty kick and somehow rose and broke through the water. Tom had an arm about her. His face was red. Somehow, they found the up-ended motorboat and clung to it until a fisherman passing by in a *banca* came to their rescue. Letty remembered lying on the bottom of the *banca*, gasping. Tom held her tight in his arms. They never went to another beach.

Letty often wondered if she had been meant to die that day. But Tom had refused to let her go. That was how she had come to marry him, that was how she had come to confuse his stubbornness for strength. Not entirely her fault: She had been 22, younger than her own son was now. She forgave her young, romantic self. She even, eventually, forgave Tom. She was sure, in spite of everything, that her life was not over. There was something yet she was meant to do. She wanted to do it. She wanted to find that thing.

Tom had become small in his middle age. Not her. She would fight. Life could still beguile, she was sure of it.

The job was only possible because it was something she could do at home. The organization was called The Bridge. There was a toll-free hotline for troubled people. The number was 1-800-U-R-SAVED. The person who had handled the late-night shift: 11 p.m. to 2 a.m., had burned out and quit. Younger people had families, or wanted to keep nights free for their partners. The job was perfect, absolutely perfect for Letty. The person who interviewed her (over the phone) said, "You know we can't pay you. This is strictly an all-volunteer organization."

"I know," Letty said. "That's fine."

Only now was she grateful for Tom's pennypinching. The money in the bank was all hers now. Even after taxes, she calculated it would be (provided she stayed healthy) enough to sustain her for several years.

And after several years?

She wouldn't think about that. She refused to think about that. She would live in the moment. She would not regret anything.

"Uh, that's great," the interviewer said. He sounded young.

The list of rules arrived in the mail three days later: ten pages, single-spaced.

Life was always, Letty mused, throwing her for a loop. Who knew that things would have turned out this well? There was simply no way to prepare for anything. One simply had to endure or proceed. And hope for the best.

"Don't despair!" she said. Letty was surprised that her voice came out sounding so trembly and wan. "There is hope!" The wife on the other end of the phone cried and said she felt stupid. She always called, around 10 p.m., when her husband had gone out.

"You're new," the wife said.

"Yes," Letty said. "But it doesn't matter. I'm here. To help you."

Her fifth caller had a terrible mother. "Pretend she doesn't exist," Letty said. "Only you. Only you are important."

The caller, a young woman (from the sound of her voice) was silent for a few moments.

"My mother doesn't exist," she said slowly, as if repeating a nursery rhyme. Then: "That's not right. Of course she exists. That's why I'm always miserable."

"Make it a game," Letty said. "Just pretend. You can do that. Anyone can play a game."

"Ok," the young woman said.

"Just try," Letty said. "You'll see."

The hardest call Letty took during the first month was from a man (middle-aged, Letty guessed) who said he suffered from Panic Disorder. The caller said the attacks had begun four years earlier.

Letty asked how the attacks usually began.

"They always start with me feeling dizzy," the caller said. "My wife says I'm probably just tired, but I'm terrified. I always wonder when the next attack will hit."

"Have you told your doctor?" Letty asked.

"No," the man said. "I have not told anyone."

"Why not?" Letty asked.

The caller hesitated a moment. "I don't know," he said.

"Don't worry so much," Letty said. "I suppose you could say I suffer from something similar. Whenever I hear the words to that Joni Mitchell song—you know, the one about a taxi? —I start to cry. I can't stop."

The man's breathing sounded funny. Then, in a low voice, he began to sing the song. Letty let him finish.

"I've bought myself a plane ticket," the man said.

"Where are you going?" Letty asked.

"San Francisco," the man said. "To throw myself off the Golden Gate Bridge."

"Don't do that," Letty said, then stopped. San Francisco! Letty had never been to San Francisco, though she longed to.

She didn't have any more words for this man, this man who wanted her to give him a reason not to go to San Francisco and throw himself off the Golden Gate Bridge.

She then broke Rule #3: she gave the caller her real name.

"How old are you?" he asked.

"I'm 48," she said, and stopped, astonished by her lie. She was constantly surprising herself, lately. But he never called again.

A week after that man, she had a call from a young girl. "Oliver's gone away," the girl sobbed. "He was married. I sneaked him into my freshman dorm for three months. My roommate promised not to tell."

Girl, Letty thought. *It's survival of the fittest.*

And then there was the husband who wanted to pull everything out of his retirement plan and spend the money traveling the world.

"Where would you go?" Letty asked.

"Morocco," the man said. "My dad went in '59. He brought back pictures of camels. After that, I'd like to go to the Ivory Coast. A friend of mine went. His wife's from Abidjan."

After they had gone back and forth for almost 10 minutes, the man's voice suddenly dropped low. "My wife won't let me, though. She won't let me go."

"Well, that's sad," Letty said. "But it's not your responsibility to keep your wife happy."

"It's not that," the man said. "But there won't be anyone to take care of her."

"And how old is your wife?" Letty asked.

"She's 44," the man said. "She's never been alone. We were married when we were both 20."

That was certainly very sad, Letty thought. Not for the wife, but for the man.

"She's not an egg," Letty said.

"Excuse me?" the man said.

"I don't mean to make light of your situation," Letty said, "but your wife's not an egg. She's not going to crack."

"I don't want to grow old," said a caller, who revealed, moments later, that she was 67.

"Being old is a state of mind," Letty said soothingly. "You'll only be old if you *feel* old. Trust me."

A caller: "I can't stop thinking of that girl in the beauty parlor. I'm 54."

Another caller: "Should I try speed-dating?"

Yet another caller: "I think I might have killed someone. Why am I telling you this?"

Caller # xx: "I don't love him anymore. But I'm afraid to tell him. Now I've started sleepwalking. Every night. Sometimes I wake up fully dressed, and there are stains on my clothing, mud all over the dining room. Why?"

Caller # xxx: "I watch my neighbors making love. They never bother closing their windows. I have them on video. I want to know how this ends."

Sometimes, the calls blurred together: "I hit my mother (Or was it my child?)"

Sometimes Letty thought it had all been a trick. "You want my advice?" she would say.

Once, during a call, she allowed her mind to wander off. She was silent. Too silent. The caller said, "Hello, are you still there?" She had no idea what the call was about.

She tried to recover. "When you get your money . . ." she began, hopefully.

"You have the brains of a fucking pigeon," the caller said, and hung up.

She allowed the obscenity to rankle inside her, for days. Weeks.

It was another dreary Saturday. Rain fell continuously. She was restless. There had only been one call all night. The man said: "Going to work is like going from one hell to another." With the recession, such calls were increasingly common.

Letters came regularly from her mother, who had never mastered e-mail. They always said the same thing: *Come home.* One of these letters had come five days earlier, on a Monday. *What kind of a life will you have there*, her mother wrote. *At least here, you can be with your family.*

As if 27 years were nothing. As if she could turn her back on all that, turn her back on her son, who though uncommunicative was still the only person in the whole world that she still loved, loved with the transparency of glass.

Absently, her gaze wandered to the bookshelf and fixed on a spiral-bound notebook, Tom's "Garden Journal." In it he would make meticulous record of the plants he had bought, and how well or how poorly they did, week by week, sometimes even day by day. He jotted down the days in which he had applied Osmocote, and how long it took for the first flower buds to appear. When he cared to, he would note particulars of the weather and observations about butterflies and birds. The first entry began 16 years and two months earlier, and the last was only two days before his first and fatal stroke.

She decided to leaf through it again now.

In the first entry for January, he had written: "Rained all day yesterday and today. Ordered six new tea roses."

In February, he wrote: "Still chilly. Dug holes, filled halfway with compost."

On 17 April, three months before his death, he wrote: "Noodle head sprinklers worthless."

Almost two months later, on the second Sunday of June, he had written: "Effective? Wait and see!" The last word was underlined twice.

A page later, Tom had written: "The righteous shall flourish like a palm tree and shall spread abroad like a cedar of Lebanon."

Letty stared at the words. They were not Tom's words, she knew. They were from the Bible. But which part? Which Gospel?

There were only five more entries after that. The roses had faded quickly, that summer. They were nothing but scraggly sticks now. Letty didn't have the time or the energy to weed and water, the way Tom did.

She recalled him fussing in the garden. What was it about his face when he was tending his beloved roses? Hope—yes, that was it. His face was filled with hope. With her he was bad-tempered, querulous, impatient. But in the garden, he was infinitely patient. Yes. He anticipated reward. He was a man of such narrow joys.

She looked through the window at the garden. Nothing was blooming out there now. She had done it. She leaned back, closed her eyes, and began, for the first time in years, to make plans.

– 0 –

ICE

Sunlight, shadows, wind. Strangely, no birds.

Out there, ice caps, cold as knives.

Steam from her mouth, his mouth, none from the boy who lay between them. She cradling the boy's face, but he knowing what.

She knowing what but not able to bear it.

Boy was the last of four. Alive just this morning. Fell through the ice chasing after a shadow that he thought was food.

What food, what a fool. There's no food on the ice. Not on top, not under.

Hadn't he told the boy over and over: Watch the sky. The food will come as a drop.

I been watching, the boy said. For weeks. I'm going blind or something.

It was true the boy's eyes were strange, as if icecaps were growing in the irises. He tried to staunch the spread, but hour by hour the ice seemed to grow. Until, he hated to say it, the boy had gone completely blind. But he still pretended to be watching the sky.

He pretended he heard something. A whirring maybe. She became quite excited and let go of the boy, just for a moment. That was when the boy ran out to the middle of the frozen lake.

Ah, too late. He wasn't fast enough to catch the boy before it was too late. The sound of the ice cracking horrified him. But at least he'd caught the boy before the breath stopped completely. At least he'd managed that.

And then he thought it was all for the best. Because then he could stop worrying about the boy and just focus. Focus on himself and her. Be glad there was still a *her*. Something he needed to remember.

Would there be any point in trying to salvage the boy's clothes. He thought, looking down at her and the boy. Not saying it out loud, of course. He hadn't gotten as bad as that.

Hallooooo, came the cry across the frozen wasteland.

What was that? He cocked his head.

Hallooooo, it came again. Over the frozen wasteland. He couldn't see very far. It was all just a blinding whiteness.

Then, a sound close, so close it made him jump.

You deaf?

It was a man. Not an old man. Not old like him. He stiffened. Put a hand down to her shoulder. But she wasn't there. Suddenly.

He was alone.

Where was the boy? Hadn't he been laid out there, right between them? Or had he imagined it all? Her and the boy? Maybe he'd been alone this whole time? Maybe this was a dream. Try jumping, his mother used to tell him when he was upset. Jump up and down, fast, 10 times. Don't stop till you reach 10.

He forced himself to move. He could barely lift his legs. He tried bending his knees. There was such pain at that moment. Maybe he'd cracked off his legs. Maybe they'd frozen and his trying to move had cracked them off.

He's messed up, the young voice said.

Sure, said another voice, young also.

He became frantic at having lost sight of her. Couldn't even see his own legs, for that matter.

How long you figure? Young Man 1 said.

Not too long, said Young Man 2. Minutes. An hour at the most.

And him? said Young Man 1.

Ah, he's no bother. Look, almost dead on his feet. Can't move. Except—there. See? He blinked.

There was a gasp. Those are tears, yeah? Look at his cheeks. This one can still cry. Think he should come with?

Ah. Why?

I haven't seen tears in a while, said Young Man 2. I can't stop looking at him. That's a sight.

What? Thinking of your Mammy, said Young Man 1.

Naw.

Yes, you are. Wuss.

Naw!

If he comes with, you've got to carry.

Young Man 1's voice was faint, as if he were already gone.

Young Man 2 did something, a clearing of the throat maybe.

Her's gone? he said.

'Fraid so, said Young Man 2.

Leave me here, he said.

Naw, said Young Man 2. You're coming with.

No, he said. Leave me here. I can't. Just take minutes. I'm almost dead already.

Naw, said Young Man 2. He felt a light touch on his arm. Then, air beneath his feet.

The world was upside down. Strange.

Am I dying, he asked. Maybe if you could wait a minute or two. Till it's over.

I'm bringing you with, said Young Man 2. No way I'm going to leave you. You got tears!

They're for her, he said.

Young Man 2 was silent for a few moments. Then he said, almost regretfully, I know.

He could get used to looking at things upside down. At least, it wasn't painful.

My mum cried, too, Young Man 2 said. That was a long time ago.

You're all that's left? he asked.

Silence. Then, yeah.

He suddenly felt heat. From a coil in his stomach? He flailed his arms.

Steady there, Young Man 2 said. We've only a little bit to go.

I've got to go back and get her, he said. Put me down.

Naw, Young Man 2 said. But he sounded regretful.

That's what you did with your own mum?

Yeah.

How'd you manage—?

Silence.

When we get to where we're going, you're going to have to put me down. Then I'm going to run back. All this for nothing. Just so you know.

Ah! said Young Man 2. It was something like a snort: I don't think so.

What? Think I won't? Watch me.

Naw, man. Youse legs are tied up.

Now that he knew, he felt the coils around his knees. Oh.

No, he said. No, no, no!

'Tis true, Young Man 2 said. No point to arguing.

You'll be dead too. Maybe tomorrow, maybe the day after. But you won't last.

I know.

So? What's the point?

The point is, there is no point.

You just keep going. Even if there's no point.

Yeah.

So brilliant.

I am, aren't I?

Not till you see the bright light. Not till then. Now, we just keep going.

$$- 0 -$$

ACKNOWLEDGMENTS

Dumaguete was published in *ms. aligned, vol. 3.*

Residents of the Deep was published in *J Journal*, Fall 2022.

Thing was published in *New Orleans Review*, Volume 38.1, 2012.

Spores was published in *decomP magazinE*, August 2016.

First Life was published in the July 18, 2015 issue of *Juked*.

First Causes was published in *Quarterly West*, Issue #89, Winter 2017.

Flight was published in *Prism International*, Winter 2012.

The Hand, winner of the *Juked Fiction Prize*, was published in *Juked*, Jan. 31, 2008.

Sofia was published in *The Hunger: A Journal*, Issue # 8 (June 1, 2020).

Down was published in *Menacing Hedge*, issue 11.02, winter/spring 2022.

The Essence of Spain was published in *Eunoia Review*, March 2014.

Appetites was published in *Café Irreal* # 31, Summer 2009.

The Elephant was published in *Your Impossible Voice*, Issue 5 (Fall 2014).

The Walker was published in *the museum of americana*, Issue 25 (October 2021).

The Future was published in *Monkeybicycle*, Aug. 12, 2016.

Samael was published in *West Branch*, Fall 2024

Don Alfredo & Jose Rizal was published in *Sou'wester*, Spring 2007.

Spinning by Candlelight was published in *The Citron Review*, Fall 2022.

Magellan's Mirror was published in *J Journal*, Fall 2012.

Toad was published in *Cleaver Magazine*, Issue 28, Winter 2020.

Sand was published in *Pembroke Magazine*, Number 53.

Bodies was published in *Vice-Versa, the Mystery Issue* (Summer/Fall, 2021).

Bridging was published in the October 2013 issue of *Waccamaw*.

ABOUT THE AUTHOR

Marianne Villanueva was born and raised in the Philippines, received a creative writing fellowship from Stanford University, and now lives in the San Francisco Bay Area. Her first story collection, *Ginseng and Other Tales from Manila*, was a finalist for the Philippines' National Book Award. Her second, *Mayor of the Roses*, was the inaugural publication of the Miami University Press Fiction Series. *Problems with Sleep*, her fifth collection, is forthcoming from Betty Books in 2026. She is writing a novel, *White Sails, Green Oceans*, about a 16th century Spanish priest who is sent to the Philippines to fight demons.

ABOUT THE PRESS

Unsolicited Press is based out of Portland, Oregon and focuses on the works of the unsung and underrepresented. As a womxn–owned, all–volunteer small publisher that doesn't worry about profits as much as championing exceptional literature, we have the privilege of partnering with authors skirting the fringes of the lit world. We've worked with emerging and award–winning authors such as Savannah Cooper, Amy Shimshon–Santo, Brook Bhagat, Elisa Carlsen, and Rosalia Scalia.

Learn more at Unsolicitedpress.com. Find us on Twitter and Instagram at @UnsolicitedP.